The Black Kettle Ride

By

Cinita Davis Brown

Illustrated by

Jean Lirley Huff

Ozark Publishing, Inc.
P.O. Box 228
Prairie Grove, AR 72753

Library of Congress cataloging-in-publication data

Brown, Cinita Davis, 1931-
    The black kettle ride / by Cinita Davis Brown ;
illustrated by Jean Lirley Huff.
        p.   cm
    Summary: In 1844 Tom Brown and his two
newborn twin daughters join other pioneer families
traveling by wagon train from Indiana to Missouri.
    ISBN 1-56763-291-2 (cloth : alk. paper). —
ISBN 1-56763-292-0 (pbk. : alk. paper)
    [1. Frontier and pioneer life—Fiction.] I. Huff,
Jean Lirley, 1946-   ill. II. Title.
PZ7.B81286B1   1997
[Fic]—dc20   96-27665
                                                  CIP
                                                  AC

Printed in the United States of America

Dedicated with love to my family.
My beloved husband, Logan
Our children, Keith (1959–1992), Lynne, and Jane
Our grandchildren, Andrew Brown and Logan and
Lucas Chrislaw

Foreword

Tom Brown lived in Brown County, Indiana, in 1844. His wife, Katie, died on Christmas Day and left him with two newborn twin daughters. Tom and several other pioneer families traveled by wagon train to Ozark County, Missouri, to start a new life. Tom took his big black kettle on the journey, giving his infant daughters a safe place to ride in the wagon.

Contents

One	Christmas Day 1844	1
Two	A Long, Lonely Winter	7
Three	A Time of Decision	13
Four	Planning for a Move	19
Five	A Trip to Nashville	25
Six	Time Flies	31
Seven	The Hamptons' Surprise	41
Eight	Tom's Purchase	49
Nine	Saying Goodbye	55
Ten	On the Road	67
Eleven	Goodbye to Nashville	75
Twelve	Wagons West	83
Thirteen	The Mississippi Behind Us	91
Fourteen	A Family Reunion	101
Fifteen	A Blacksmith Shop in the Ozarks	107
Sixteen	The Year of 1845 Ends	113

Chapter 1

Christmas Day 1844

Christmas morning came to Brown County, Indiana, in 1844. Cold, cold temperatures moved down from the north that Christmas morning and rested a heavy hand there.

Christmas morning came to the log cabin on Salt Creek in Brown County where Thomas S. Brown lived with his wife, Margaret Davis Brown. Thomas affectionately called his young wife "Katie," and she called him "Tom." They had married in June of 1842.

Christmas morning came to Tom and Katie's cabin, but it brought no "Christmas Joy" . . . no joy, only fear. Fear of such magnitude that it caused Tom to wonder if the Angel of old had really proclaimed, "Fear not; for behold I bring you good tidings of great joy . . ." Tom pondered and thought. His mind wondered. He was filled with fear . . . stark, unmasked fear! Fear from which there seemed no escape.

Katie was expecting their first child in late February. But it seemed "her time" had come on Christmas Eve. Her time had come two months earlier than it should have. She had "labored" hard throughout the long, cold Christmas Eve night . . . labored throughout all Christmas Day, and still, the baby was not born.

Old Granny Fleetwood, one of the best "granny women" in the hills of Brown County, was there to help Katie. She had helped bring many a babe into the world.

Hannah Todd, younger and not as experienced, was there, too. She was ready to help with the birthin' . . . to learn more about being a good "granny woman" from Granny Fleetwood. Both women wanted to help Katie. Both women wished they could help bear some of Katie's pain, for it was the custom of these pioneers to bear each other's burdens. They did all they could, all they knew how to do. Still the labor continued and the baby would not, could not, be born. Tom carried wood and kept water heating over the roaring fire in the fireplace. These chores he could do. He could not help

2

Katie. He could not dispel his fear. Tom asked himself, "Will this baby die? Die before it really lives?"

He tried to block out a more frightening thought. "Could his beloved Katie also die?"

Tom fought his fear—fought . . . and lost the battle. He let his mind wander, willing it to think of other Christmases that had come and gone. Other Christmases in this very same little cabin in the hills of Brown County.

As Tom thought, he relived his past in his mind. He remembered his first marriage . . . his first young bride, Sarah Floyd, whom he had married almost five years ago. "Yes," he told himself, "come January twenty-sixth, it would be exactly five years since his marriage to Sarah, whom he always called 'Sally.'" He smiled to himself as he remembered sometimes calling her "Sally" . . . "my Sally Goodin." He and Sarah had married in January of 1839. By summer of that year they were in their own cabin which neighbors had helped Tom build. He smiled as he remembered the "log rolling" and the "cabin raising." The cabin was sound, snug, and warm. The corn crop matured and was gathered. Hunting was good. All was well. All was well except Sarah. She had suffered from fever and chills all spring, all summer, and on into the fall.

Before Thanksgiving they knew that Sarah was with child. By early summer they would have their first baby. "She would feel better then," they told themselves.

3

But, in late April of 1840 Tom buried his young wife holding their baby. Buried them on a hill near their cabin . . . the cabin he now shared with his second wife, his Katie.

Tom thought. He pondered. Another tear slid from his eyes. He remembered that with Sarah and the baby, he had buried many of his dreams. The same dreams most young frontier men dreamed during the early 1840s . . . dreams of a good wife in a snug cabin, dreams of a baby in a cradle by the fireplace, dreams of good hunting, a good corn crop.

Tom's dreams were lofty dreams, and though he buried them for a time, life went on around him. He remembered that other settlers had come in slowly and located, for the most part, on the hills of the area. By 1836, enough settlers had arrived to warrant the formation of a new county. Tom was there; he remembered. This was history in the making. History of a new land, of a new county . . . Brown County. Tom swelled with pride as he thought, "I am part of this new land, part of the history of this land."

Much work needed to be done in this new land. Work that must be completed to make the county really livable . . . a place to rear a family. Roads needed to be built. Tom helped with this. A covered bridge needed to be built. Tom helped. He remembered all this.

Most of his neighbors had children. The Hamptons, Ayers, Tabors, Noblets, Hollens, Williamsons, and even some of his own people, the Browns, had children.

Children needed to know how to read and write and how to figure. They needed a log schoolhouse. Tom helped build it. He remembered.

The new land, a new county, needed a church . . . a strong, sturdy log structure. Tom helped cut the logs, build the church, split logs for the pews for the church that they called the Shiloh Methodist Church. Yes, he remembered. He thought and pondered as he remembered all this.

Tom thought of the time at that church when it seemed that God was speaking directly to him, saying, "Preach my Word. I need laborers in this new land." Tom answered God's call. He was doing the best he could to carry the Gospel. He pondered and remembered . . . and could not keep himself from again shedding a few tears.

It seemed as if Tom's entire life had flashed before his eyes . . . thirty years of life, for he had been born in 1814 in Virginia.

He was remembering, pondering . . . thinking, remembering . . . pondering some more. As long as he could think of the past, he did not have to face the present . . . Christmas Day 1844. He could escape his fear for a moment. He did not have to wonder, "How much longer can my little Katie endure this agony? What, oh what, is wrong? Why can't this baby be born? Oh, if only there was a doctor that I could fetch!"

He prayed silently, "God in Heaven, on this day, this Christmas Day, I recall the birth of another baby. A baby born in a stable. Both Mother Mary and the baby survived that cold, harsh, stable birth. God in Heaven, please help my Katie bring this baby into the world. Please help my Katie. Please let this baby be born now." He pleaded. He prayed.

Suddenly, from across the cabin, the sound of a baby's cry interrupted Tom's prayer. That sound jarred him from reliving the past and thrust him into the present . . . late afternoon of Christmas Day 1844.

His voice froze in his throat. He was afraid to look toward the bed. His arms ached for his Katie . . . for his baby. He had heard its cry! He must not go to the bed. Must not chance getting in the way. Tom stoked the fire. He wondered, worried . . . could not let go of his fear . . . could not allow himself to be filled with hope.

The old clock, the one that Katie took such pride in, sat on the mantle in its place by the Bible. It slowly ticked the seconds away. Seconds seemed like hours.

Finally he heard Granny Fleetwood say, "This baby girl is small, oh, so small, but she has a good color and a strong cry. I think . . ." Suddenly, Hannah Todd's voice interrupted. "Lord, help us! Look! Another baby's coming."

Granny Fleetwood looked. A second baby, another girl, was born. She, too, announced her arrival with a welcomed cry.

And on that night, that Christmas night in 1844, Katie, Tom's beloved Katie, died.

Chapter 2

A Long, Lonely Winter

Tom's first thoughts were those of denial. "It can't be. Katie can't be dead. Not again! Not another cold mound on the lonely, wind-swept hill. Not another sandstone. Not another task of carving the name BROWN in that stone. It simply can't be. It can't be true. My Katie can't be dead."

Then he heard the sound . . . the sound of first one baby and then another one. Babies crying. His babies. His and Katie's twin babies. Babies who would never feed at their mother's breast. Babies who would never hear a lullaby from their mother's lips. They were his babies. He was solely responsible for them now . . . totally and completely responsible.

They must have names. They were so tiny, so helpless. Could they possibly survive? Survive without a mother? A name would make them seem more real. The firstborn, she was so tiny, and yet she seemed stronger. Tom named her Julia Anna. The other one, even smaller, he called Margaret Emily. Big names, strong names for such tiny babies.

The next day Tom buried their mother, his child-bride, his beloved Katie. He buried her on the hill near their cabin, by the side of Sarah Floyd Brown and the baby who had died without even having a name.

Tom wept. Then he turned his back to the graves and headed toward the cabin, the cabin where Julia

Anna and Margaret Emily slept. Christmas of 1844 was past. A new year was upon him. He had decisions to

make, work to be done, twin daughters to care for, to raise without the help of a mother.

When Tom had time for thinking, remembering, he pondered on things he and Katie had done to get ready for winter . . . things Katie had done to prepare for the arrival of their baby. He thought, "Did she ever think that she would have twins? Oh, she would have been so proud! So proud of her tiny Julia Anna and Margaret Emily."

Katie had insisted back in early fall that Tom swap for a young heifer. The heifer had calved on Thanksgiving Day, so there was milk for the twins. "One less worry," Tom thought.

The twins seemed so fragile, so tiny. Tom wished he could weigh them. He felt sure that each one of them weighed less than four pounds. Love—he felt it in every fiber of his body as he looked at his tiny babies. Oh, how he wished that he could share the joy of parenthood with Katie.

Tom felt love and joy as he looked at his tiny girls, sorrow and emptiness as he thought of his Katie, fear and uncertainty as he asked himself, "How can I raise these babies, these precious, precious little girl babies, by myself?"

Slowly, slowly the cold dark days of 1844 ended, and a new year was upon the little cabin and its occupants.

Tom was busy and watchful as he cared for his babies, his Julia Anna and Margaret Emily. The cow was kept close to the door of the cabin. When the babies were hungry, he milked the cow and fed the babies her fresh, warm milk.

Sadly Tom remembered chiding his Katie as she had sat by the fireplace during the autumn evenings . . . sat there dreaming and spinning or stitching on clothes for the baby she was carrying. He remembered saying, "Katie, that baby won't need so many clothes, so many blankets, so many diapers." There was enough for two babies, and he was thankful . . . one less worry for him now.

Tom was grateful for the warm, fresh milk the cow provided for the babies. He did not have to think about clothes for them for a while. Plenty of wood for the fireplace was already cut, and he had enough food for himself. Yes, they could make do for a time. Later he would have to make a decision. He needed to think and plan carefully. He must pray for wisdom and guidance as he planned for their future.

Chapter 3

A Time of Decision

The long, dark, cold days of January and February slowly passed. By mid-March Tom could see a serviceberry tree blooming on the hill near Katie's and Sally's graves. Robins were busy all around the cabin as they staked their claims to their new nesting sites. Spring was in the air.

Julia Anna and Margaret Emily were almost three months old. As Tom gazed at them, he could scarcely believe his eyes. They were healthy babies and had grown so fast. He held them by the hour and drew comfort from their nearness. Each of them could bring a tear of joy to Tom's eyes as they looked at him so trustingly. When they wrapped one of their tiny hands around his big, rough, work-worn fingers, he thought his heart would burst. He felt so much love and protectiveness for his girls, and he missed their mother, his precious little Katie, so much. He sat by the hour watching the babies and studied each move, each change in their expressions. They were so alike in looks that only Tom could tell them apart, and yet, he could tell they were distinctly different.

As Tom moved about the cabin he could see their little black eyes following him. He felt certain they recognized him. "Pa" he called himself to them. How the sound of that little word, even in his own voice, thrilled him!

A childless couple, the Hamptons, lived over on the other side of Salt Creek. They had visited Tom and the twins almost daily during those long winter months. Tom would say, "Hannah, I don't know what I would do without your help." Hannah Hampton loved holding the babies. She ached for a baby of her own. Her husband, Hiram, watched Hannah as she busied herself helping Tom care for Julia Anna and Margaret Emily. As Hiram watched his wife and saw the longing in her face, he, too, wished with all his heart that they could have a baby.

Hiram and Hannah had spent long hours discussing Tom and the twins. "How can he raise them by himself?" they asked. They had an idea, a plan. They told themselves that they only wanted to help . . . to do what would be best for the babies . . . to be neighborly . . . to help Tom.

Late in March Tom seemed depressed. Hiram and Hannah could sense his loneliness, his frustration. It seemed the time was right to approach Tom with their plan. Tom listened attentively as Hiram said, "You know that Hannah and I have been married for over ten years now and still have no children. We've about given up hope of having our own baby, so we've been talking, Tom. You know, you said to us that you don't know how you'll manage when spring comes and you have to get out of the cabin and start the crops. Well, Hannah and I were wondering . . . would you let us take the twins and raise them as our own? You know that we love them and would always be good to them. We would let you—"

"NO, NO, NO, NEVER!" Tom's voice interrupted Hiram.

Both Hiram and Hannah saw that Tom was very upset. Hiram finally spoke, "Tom, we didn't mean to hurt you. We know how hard you've tried with the babies . . . how much you miss Katie. We just thought—"

Again Tom interrupted Hiram. "I know you meant well, that you just want to help. You are good, kind people. You've been so good to me . . . to my babies. You were good friends to Katie. But you must understand! Julia Anna and Margaret Emily are my babies, my flesh and blood, my responsibility! They must be raised by me or by people of their own blood. I could never let anyone else take them to raise—not even you, my good friends and neighbors. No, no, no, a thousand times no. I will raise them. Their Grandmother Davis has moved on out west to Missouri, and we'll go there. She will help me with them. That's what Katie would want me to do."

Hannah hugged and kissed both of the babies, and she and Hiram went on home to their own cabin, fearing that they had greatly upset Tom. After they left, Tom squared his shoulders and drew himself up to his full six-feet height. His black eyes were bright and clear, and his short whiskered chin was set in a determined look. The worried facial expression that he had worn most of the time since Katie's death faded into a peaceful, determined look.

Tom was talking to himself, but he spoke aloud. "Well, friends, you did me a big favor when you offered to take my girls to raise as your own. You forced me to make a decision. I have known in my own heart since Christmas Day—since the very day my Katie, their mother, died—that I must raise them myself, but I've also known that I would need help. Their grandmother will want to help with them. We need her help, must have her help, and she needs to be with her grand-daughters."

Walking to the bed where Julia Anna and Margaret Emily lay, Tom gazed intently at them and said, "Girls, we've got a long ride ahead of us. We are moving to the Ozarks, to Missouri, to be near your Grandma Davis. But, first there's a lot of work that I've got to do."

Tom's heart felt lighter, more free of burden than it had for weeks. He walked to the cabin door and threw it open. Breathing deeply, he filled his lungs with fresh, spring air. Looking to the south he saw a flock of wild geese. They formed a perfect "V" in the sky as they flew north with haunting cries. They were on their way to their summer home. Tom felt that seeing them at this time—the time when he had finally reached a definite decision—was a good omen.

Chapter 4

Planning for a Move

Early the following morning before the twins were awake, Tom sat in front of the fireplace drinking a cup of strong, steaming coffee and reading his Bible. As he read he felt a new peace, a contentment he had not felt since Katie's death. He read, "And I will give you peace in the land . . . and none shall make you afraid."

From the door came the sound of a soft tap, tap, tapping. At first Tom thought it was only the wind, but as he listened he knew it was someone knocking softly on the door of his cabin. The latchstring had been pulled inside of the door the evening before, so Tom lifted the latch and opened the cabin's door.

A tired, sorrowful-looking Hiram Hampton stood in the doorway. "Come on in, Hiram," Tom said softly enough to not wake the babies. "Have a chair, and I'll fetch you a cup of coffee."

Tom returned with the coffee for Hiram and then sat down in his own chair.

Hiram raised his head, looked into Tom's eyes, and said, "Tom, Hannah and I have been sick with worry since we left here yesterday. We never meant to sound as if we thought you couldn't or wouldn't care for the twins . . . that you don't love them. We just . . ."

Tom interrupted him, saying, "Hiram, my

friend, God bless you and your good wife. Stop your worrying. I was not offended by your offer to take my babies . . . to raise my girls. If I did not feel that I could, that I must, raise them myself, I can think of no one who would be better or more loving parents than you and Hannah. No, no, no, Hiram, I'm not upset with you. In fact, you did me a big favor. You forced me to face my options . . . to choose my destiny . . . to make a decision. I must get the babies near their grandmother."

Tom paused and took a sip of his coffee. He looked toward the west corner of the cabin, but it seemed that his mind was far away. Finally he spoke, "This land here in Indiana has claimed my two young wives. Missouri is a newer land, a wilder land. Hunting is good there. The water is pure, and the land is easy to get. The area is made up of forest-covered hills, ridges, and valleys much like the land here in southern Indiana. Katie and I had talked about going. I feel that I can hear her saying, 'Yes, Tom, you've made the right choice. Get to Missouri, near my ma. Go just as soon as you can.'"

Hiram thought about what Tom had said, and then he said, "Well, if Hannah and I can help you in any way, you know that we will."

"You can. You can help me today. I need Hannah to care for Julia Anna and Margaret Emily for a few days while I get ready to make the long journey. I have so much to do. You know, Hiram, several people from right around here in Brown County have already moved to the area of Missouri that they call the Ozarks. Among them were the Fleetwoods, Hicks, Rippees, Stouts, Todds, Brummets, and of course Katie's own Davis family. Perhaps there are others who will want to go this spring. I need to see people . . . to make plans . . . to get things ready."

Hiram stood up and said, "I'll go fetch Hannah now. We can care for the babies while you get ready."

As Hiram left the cabin Tom heard a sound and knew the babies were awake. They were happy little things, and as Tom lifted first one and then the other twin he said, "Well, my girls, you are getting to be quite an armful. Your Grandma Davis will be so surprised and happy to see you, and so will your Uncle George Washington Davis. He lives with your grandma down in the Ozarks. Your Uncle Isaac and Aunt Elizabeth live near your grandma and your Uncle George. Uncle Isaac married your Aunt Elizabeth here in Brown County. They had a baby boy, William, before they left Indiana and went to Missouri. Probably have more kids by now, so you'll have scads of cousins to play with in your new home."

Julia Anna and Margaret Emily made soft cooing sounds and smiled at Tom. He thought, "They can't possibly understand me, and yet, their pleased smiles make me wonder. Oh, Katie, how I wish you could be here! If only you could make this move with us, how happy I'd be!"

Tom had the warm fresh milk ready for the

babies before they awoke, so the early feeding went smoothly. Before Tom had finished bathing and dressing both babies, Hannah and Hiram were at the cabin. "Let me do that, Tom," Hannah said.

Tom laughingly said, "Be happy to. I guess I've learned a lot, but I still feel so awkward and clumsy when I handle my girls. Sure seems that my hands fit a plow handle or a sledgehammer better than a baby. And, oh my cooking, I sometimes wonder if I will be able to eat it! You know you brought me that fat young squirrel yesterday, Hiram. Well, I cooked it for my supper last night, and when I tried to eat it, I wondered if it could have been a skunk. Whew, my cooking! Just don't know how you women do it so easily, Hannah."

All three of them laughed. Hiram and Hannah saw how much more relaxed and happy Tom seemed. They thought, "This is the first time we've seen Tom laugh, really laugh, since Katie died."

Hannah was busy caring for the twins, and Tom prepared to leave the cabin. Before he left, he kissed both babies and told Hannah, "I'm going into Nashville to start buying supplies for the journey. Today I'll see if I can get wagon sheeting to cover the wagon. The girls must have a covered wagon to travel in. It must be snug and dry. I can make the bows out of green hickory strips. The wagon at the blacksmith shop is in good shape. We can travel in it after I cover it and fix it up."

Thoughts of the trip filled Tom's mind. He continued talking excitedly. "I also want to see if I can find anyone from around here who is heading west to Missouri this spring. I have lots to do, lots to see about, so I don't know when I'll return."

Hannah replied, "Take your time. Hiram and I will take Julia Anna and Margaret Emily on home with us. We'll take care of them until you get back. Don't you worry about them for one minute."

Tom went out of the cabin to his blacksmith shop. When he entered it to get his saddle and bridle, he breathed deeply. The blacksmith odors—the smell of charcoal, leather, and horses—all blended together and made Tom realize just how much he had missed spending time in his shop.

Tom ran his hands over his leather apron. He thought, "I am a blacksmith, a smithy, but I know that my services will be needed in the Ozarks, too. I am a smithy first of all, but I can do many things. I can make the shoes and put them on a horse or an ox, but I can be a wheelwright, a harness maker, a cooper, or a tanner. I can also be a carpenter when a coffin needs to be made quickly. And then, I can help carry the Word, help marry the young, and bury the dead. Surely I am needed in the new land called the Ozarks. Surely God and His people can use me there. Yes, Missouri . . . Ozarks . . . here comes Tom Brown and his twin girls."

Chapter 5

A Trip to Nashville

It took longer than usual for Tom to reach Nashville. He lived about ten miles south of the little town that was the county seat of Brown County, Indiana. This was his first trip into town since he had buried his Katie.

News traveled slowly in the 1840s in the sparsely settled area of Brown County where Tom lived. In spite of this, almost everyone that he saw along the trail to Nashville had heard of the birth of the twins and of Katie's death. Everyone he met wanted to talk . . . to hear about the twins. They said, "How are you doing? How are the babies? We were so sorry to hear about Katie." So Tom visited along the road as he made his way into Nashville.

It was almost dark when he finally arrived there. He tied his horse to a hitching post near the jail. The jail was built of hewn logs. The walls of the jail were double, and each was one foot thick. The space between the logs was filled with hewed lumber inserted perpendicularly.

Tom looked at the jail and thought, "I helped with this structure when it was built in 1837. The iron bars that form the door and the iron grills over the windows came from my blacksmith shop. I made them. No

prisoner has escaped from this place."

His thoughts went from the jail to his babies. He said to himself, "Girls, this is the first night since you were born that I haven't tucked you into bed, wrapped you each in that old soft quilt that your mama so lovingly made, said a prayer over you and for you. "Oh, God, do protect my babes. Let me be what I should be as a father. Be with us . . . Go with us to our new home.'"

While Tom was lost in thought and prayer, John Floyd, his former father-in-law, came out of the courthouse that was near the jail. He eagerly greeted Tom and insisted that he go home with him. "Hester will not forgive me if I tell her that I saw you and didn't fetch you home for supper and to stay all night. You can get on about your business early in the morning."

At the mention of supper, Tom remembered Hester Floyd's good cooking. He suddenly realized how hungry and tired he was. He knew that the Floyds would know if any of the people from around Nashville planned to move west during the spring or summer of 1845.

Tom untied his horse, and leading it, he walked along with John to the Floyds' home. Hester greeted them at the door. She hugged Tom and said, "Oh, Tom, sometimes it seems life is so unfair. First you lost Sally and then Katie. How are you and the twins doing? I heard they are both girls."

Tom answered, "Well, we are getting by. The twins . . . I named them Julia Anna and Margaret Emily . . . they're growing every day. The Hamptons kept them so I could come into Nashville for supplies. If I can find anyone else who plans to go this spring, I'll take the girls and move to Missouri."

"If you'd move into Nashville, Tom, maybe I could help take care of the babies," Hester said.

"I appreciate that offer, and I'll make sure that you get to see my babies soon," Tom said proudly.

The aroma of cooking foods, a good fresh meaty smell mingled with a spicy molasses smell, greeted Tom. He smiled as he remembered his own feeble attempts at cooking for himself over the last few months. He certainly was anticipating a meal at Hester

27

Floyd's table again. He was happy to hear her say, "Well, I'll put an extra plate on the table. John, you and Tom wash up and let's eat."

After supper the three of them sat by the fireplace and talked of the things going on around Nashville. Tom listened to John and Hester, even joined the conversation. But, he was surprised to find that he could not concentrate. He did not know what was being said. His mind was back at his cabin with his little black-eyed Julia Anna and Margaret Emily. He wondered, "Do they miss me? I must hurry tomorrow and get on home before dark . . . get back to my babies."

Hester saw that Tom was weary. She fixed a bed for him, and they all went to bed. Tom had been up since five o'clock that morning and needed to get up early again tomorrow for his day in Nashville. As he tried to sleep, he found himself listening for the sound of a baby. Finally he slept. He was surprised when John Floyd said, "Tom, it's six A.M. and Hester has breakfast ready."

After a hearty breakfast, Tom thanked Hester and promised to bring the twins for her to see before he left the area. He left the Floyds' home and went to Brummet's General Store where he bought twenty square yards of heavy canvas that was called "wagon sheeting."

Tom was surprised to see that Nashville had grown during the past few months when he had not been into town. It was a bustling, thriving community. He thought to himself, "I'm glad I'm moving farther west. Think I'm a pioneer at heart. I need new lands, fresh hunting, new streams to explore. I enjoy meeting new people. Yes, I must move this summer."

By midmorning Tom had talked to several men, including Jackson Fleetwood, who said that he planned to take his family and move to the Ozarks when weather conditions were right. Jackson knew of other families, the Rippees, Hoppers, and possibly the Carsons, who also planned to head west come spring.

Jackson was a huge man. His height and weight made Tom feel small. As he listened to Jackson, Tom thought, "He looks like he just got back from a bear hunt . . . maybe a bear hunt where his only weapon was a club."

Tom looked at Jackson's bushy, dark brown hair and at his face which was covered with curly whiskers. He could scarcely see his eyes. He laughed and said, "Jackson, did anyone ever call you Bear?"

Jackson said, "Not many people would dare, but I would not mind that as a nickname if it came from you, Tom." The two of them laughed together and agreed to meet back in Nashville on Thursday of the next week. Jackson was to notify the other families who were interested in moving to Missouri. Perhaps they could all travel together.

Tom told Jackson, "I must be in a group to travel . . . sort of a wagon train. I don't dare start alone. I will need help with the babies. I plan to do my part, carry my weight, but you never know what can happen on a journey such as this. I'm sure we will be traveling five hundred miles or more. I just can't take chances with my little girls. I need some woman in the group to watch over them while I care for the horses and animals that we will take along. I hate to ask for help, to be beholden to anyone, but, I can't, won't, neglect my girls. And, speaking of my girls, I need to load my wagon sheeting on my pack horse and head home to them. See you next Thursday, Jackson."

The trip home took less time than the trip to Nashville had taken. Before dark Tom was back at the Hamptons' cabin. How happy he was to see Julia Anna and Margaret Emily. Hannah insisted that he eat supper with Hiram and her before taking the girls and going home. The Hamptons were eager to know of Tom's plans for the move and to hear news from Nashville.

Chapter 6

Time Flies

Tom had been away from the twins only a couple of days, but he was so happy to be back in his own cabin with them. He knew that he should tuck them into bed. Instead of doing this, he sat down and held them both on his lap. He felt such happiness that he sang—

My Julia Anna is a black-eyed babe
My Margaret E's the same

They're the sweetest little girls
That ever had a name.

The babies sensed Tom's carefree, jovial mood and spread big grins on their little faces. He looked at them and said, "Listen to that old hoot owl, girls. He's not saying, "Who-o-o, who-o-o, who-o-o-'r-you?' Hear him? Tonight he's saying, 'Moo-o-o, moo-o-o, move-to the-Ozzzarks.' He's hooting just for us tonight."

The twins continued to smile as they made their

baby sounds, "Goo, goo, goo." It seemed they were doing the harmony for the old owl's song.

Tom laughed out loud, slapped his knees, and laughed again, long and loudly. Then he began talking to the babies. They looked at him, and he said, "Yes, girls, we will be ready to move to Missouri very soon. It's the thing we must do. The only sorrow, real regret, that I have is that we will leave the grave of your dear mama here in the soil of Brown County. You'll never get to pick a wild rose and put it on her grave."

Thinking of Katie and how she loved wild roses brought tears to Tom's eyes. He snuggled the babies closer to himself and to each other.

He continued talking . . . almost whispering as he said, "Yes, her grave will be left here, but her spirit, her love, will go with us, will be with you all of your lives. We must move to Missouri. You must grow up knowing your mama's people, especially your grandma."

Tom sat holding both babies, sat there pondering, remembering, thinking, and planning. He found himself praying. Soon he realized that both babies were asleep, so he tucked them into bed. He came back to his chair, and though he was tired, he sat there instead of going to bed. His mind was full and busy . . . full of memories of the past and busy with plans for the future. Finally, long after the babies were asleep and the old owl had quit hooting, Tom went to bed. He slept little that night.

The following morning Hiram and Hannah Hampton were at Tom's cabin just as the sun peeked over the eastern horizon. Hannah's red hair, which she said came from her Irish grandfather, had been slicked back into a bun. Curls crept out all around her face.

Freckles dotted her nose, and her eyes twinkled with laughter. She looked more like a schoolgirl than a pioneer housewife who would soon celebrate her thirtieth birthday.

Hiram was shorter and heavier than Tom. His black hair was sprinkled with gray and was getting thin. No one had ever called him a handsome man.

When the Hamptons arrived at Tom's cabin, Hannah looked at the twins. Her whole being seemed to become warm, loving, and caring. Hiram watched his wife, and he too looked happier, more caring. Hiram and Hannah cared deeply for each other. Both of them loved Julia Anna and Margaret Emily almost as much as if they were their own.

Hiram spoke to Tom, saying, "Well, Tom, Hannah and I have reached a decision. We're going to Missouri . . . to the land you call the Ozarks . . . going with you, the girls, and the others."

Hannah hastily added, "We came early so that I can take care of the babies. You two go on and do what needs to be done. Get to work on the wagons. I'll have dinner ready for you at noon. Now, scat. Go and let me get on with my work. I've brought some dried apples to cook, and I'll make a pie if I have time."

Tom threw back his head, laughed, and said, "Don't get too busy for that." Then he and Hiram headed for the blacksmith shop.

Hannah was busy all morning with the babies and her cooking. She did find time to air Katie's good quilts. She knew Tom would take them with him. He knew how proud Katie was of them . . . how much they meant to her.

Hannah thought about Katie. She looked at the twins and said, "Yes, your mama's quilts and her clock must go to your new home. Your pa would never think of leaving them behind."

Hannah heard the bark of Brownie, Tom's faithful old hound dog. She knew that Hiram and Tom were on their way back to the cabin for dinner. She had been so busy that time had passed quickly. It seemed impossible that it was already noon. The dried-apple pie had been made and had baked in the Dutch oven. It was cooling on the table. A pone of corn bread was cooking in the Dutch oven. She smiled to herself, remembering when she was a young bride ten years before. What a

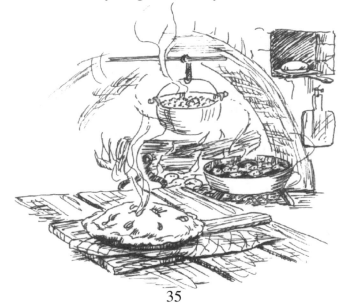

time she had learning to bake corn pone! The crusts on many a batch had been burned. She could almost smell burned corn pone as she remembered. She laughed aloud as she thought of Hiram saying, "Don't fret. We'll eat it anyhow. The burned part is good for the bellyache."

She was happy that her cooking skills had improved. She smiled as she looked at the dried-apple pie with its nicely browned crust. The iron dinner pot simmered over the coals in the fireplace. It was full of beans cooked with a big chunk of cured, smoked ham. Potatoes baked in the hot ashes near the front of the fireplace. She peeled a few onions that were left from last summer's garden. She smiled and spoke to the babies. "This meal will fill those two hungry men . . . fill them to the brim, and there'll be plenty of it left over for your pa's supper."

Hannah removed the coals from the top of the Dutch oven. The corn pone was done to perfection. The cabin door burst open, and an excited Tom and Hiram entered. They spoke at once, saying, "We found a bee tree! We found a bee tree!"

A bee tree was sure to yield honey that both families needed. Honey was their main source of sweetening. Hannah appreciated their enthusiasm, but she said, "Upon my word! Don't tell me you two have traipsed through the woods all morning hunting a bee tree. You were supposed to be working, getting ready to head west."

Tom eyed the pie while Hiram explained. "Now, Hannah, we were working. We went down by the creek hunting just the right size hickory sapling. We must have green hickory to make the bows for the wagon."

Tom interrupted him and said, "We found and cut some dandy ones, too. This afternoon we'll trim and bark those saplings and shape the bows. Tomorrow we'll start covering my wagon."

Hannah's eyes danced, and she said, "Well, I'm glad you were taking care of the job that you set out to do."

"But, let us tell you about our morning," Hiram said. "We were heading down to the bottom when we heard the drumming call of prairie chickens."

Tom added, "Seemed as if they were announcing to us . . . to all of Indiana . . . that spring had come to stay. Birds sang in the bushes, and a flock of ducks passed overhead on their way north."

Hannah was caught up in the excitement of spring and of a "possible secret" which she had been savoring to herself . . . a secret which seemed too good to be true. She would share this secret with Hiram first, and then they would share it with Tom. She said, "I noticed that the forests and hills have a green cast now. I saw a few Johnnie-jump-ups blooming when I went to the spring for water yesterday."

"Yes, that's why we found the bee tree," Tom explained. "We were down by Salt Creek where the pussy willows are in flower. Well, we heard this buzzing, and sure enough, honey bees were busy all over the place. You know how bees do," he continued. "They'd buzz all around those fuzzy little pussy willow buds and then rise in the air and fly around in circles as if trying to decide which way to go."

Hiram smiled at Tom's description and added, "We got to watching, and it seemed they made a beeline up toward the top of a certain big old oak tree. Sure enough, it's hollow. The bees were busy, busy, busy! In and out. In and out. Oh, I bet that tree is full of honey!"

Hannah said, "Well, are we going to talk or eat?"

Tom walked over to the bed where the babies were lying. He said, "Were you good girls for Hannah this morning? Looks like she has a splendid dinner ready. I sure am hungry! I'll hold you after we eat." Both babies laughed aloud. It seemed as if they "oooed and gooed" in concert just for their pa.

While Tom and Hiram washed up, Hannah dished up the meat and beans and fished the baked potatoes out of the hot ashes. As she put them on the table, she said, "Ouch, hot as a baked potato, for sure!"

Tom and Hiram laughed as they sat down at the table. Hannah sat on the bench by Hiram. Tom took them both by the hands, bowed his head, and said, "Our Father, for the many good things that come to us from Thy bounty, we give Thee thanks. For my precious babies and their good health . . . for these friends and their help and concern . . . for food, a bee tree, and an apple pie . . . we give Thee thanks. Amen."

After eating, Tom and Hiram went back to the woods, taking buckets and axes with them. If they worked quickly, they would have time to make and shape the wagon bows and to cut the bee tree.

Hannah cared for Julia Anna and Margaret Emily. While she busied herself about the cabin, she dreamed about her "secret." She smiled and thought, "Tonight I'll tell Hiram."

At dusk Tom and Hiram returned with buckets full of fresh honey in its comb. They reported that the hickory bows were ready to go on the wagon the next morning.

Hiram and Hannah went on to their cabin. Tom was anxious to spend the evening with his babies. How happy he was that supper was ready to eat!

Chapter 7

The Hamptons' Surprise

Tom was awakened the next morning by the sound of the wind. He went to the cabin door and opened it. The wind was warm and blowing from the southwest. He looked toward the twins' bed and saw that they were both awake. He said to them, "Just listen to that wind, girls. Hear it? 'Rush, rush, rush,' it seems to be saying to me."

Before Tom finished feeding the babies and eating his own breakfast, Hiram and Hannah arrived. Tom saw the look of total happiness on each of their faces. He smiled to himself as he looked at them. Hiram said, "Tom, do we have some news . . . an announcement . . . for you! Hannah is going to have a baby—a baby! Can you believe it? After all these years . . . a baby of our own!"

Tom was speechless . . . for one of the few times in his life . . . completely speechless for a moment. He put an arm around Hannah's shoulders and slapped Hiram on the back. The three of them had tears streaming down their cheeks. Finally Tom said, "Oh, the joys of being a parent!"

Hiram said, "We talked most of the night. Hannah still wants to go to Missouri with you and the girls, but I refuse to chance having her travel now.

Maybe we'll come next spring . . . not now, though."

Hannah went to the bed and picked up the babies while Tom got Hiram a cup of coffee. They talked for a time. Then Tom said, "I'll miss you both. So will the girls, but our plans can't change. We must get to the Ozarks."

"Oh yes, we know that," Hiram said.

Hannah quickly added, "And we're here to help you. We'll do all we can to get you three on the road. So scat, you two. Time's a'wasting. Talking won't cover that wagon."

Tom and Hiram left the cabin for a morning's work. At noon they reported that the bows were firmly attached to the wagon, and they were stretching the canvas.

Tom smiled as Hiram told Hannah, "You know Tom. Everything must be done just so-so. Of course, his

wagon, tools, and harness are already in tiptop shape. All we have to do is get the wagon covered."

Tom said, "Well, I've always tried to live by the Golden Rule and two other old sayings. 'A job worth doing is worth doing well,' and 'A place for everything and everything in its place.'"

Tom and his listeners laughed, and Tom continued, "I know that's not Scripture—guess it didn't even come from Ben Franklin's Almanac, but I've always found them good rules to live by."

Hannah said, "Right, so let's get to doing those jobs well."

Hiram smiled but grumbled as he said, "Tom, that wife of mine thinks we are workhorses. We may as well go on and get to work."

By evening the wagon was covered and ready for the trip. Tom and Hiram looked at it with pride. Tom said, "It doesn't look like a real Conestoga fresh from the factory in Pennsylvania, but it's not too bad for a couple of Indiana plowboys."

Hiram replied, "It's a good job, Tom. Should keep the twins and your supplies snug and dry on your long journey to Missouri."

After one more inspection of the newly covered wagon, Tom and Hiram put their tools back in the blacksmith shop. Then they headed to the cabin. Just before they opened the door, they turned around for another look at the wagon. Tom's old hound dog had managed to get up in the wagon. His head was sticking out of the

back where the canvas had been brought together form-
ing an upside-down U. His impatient-sounding bark
seemed to say, "What about me? Am I to be left here, or
do I go to Missouri with you? Seems as if you've forgot-

ten me and hunting since the babies got here." He threw
back his head and with a loud, "Yooo, yooo, yooo,
yooowl," registered his protest at being neglected by Tom.

Hiram and Tom laughed at the old hound's
antics and then went on into the cabin. Hannah was

happy to see them. She loved caring for the twins and talked or sang to them almost constantly. She enjoyed her time with Julia Anna and Margaret Emily, but it was good to be part of grown-up conversation, too. She wanted to know about the plans and preparations for the move. Life was busy and exciting around the Browns' cabin.

Tom said, "Tomorrow is Thursday. That's the day I'm to meet Jackson back at Nashville, the day we set to plan for our journey to the Ozarks."

Hannah said, "Tom, you know you don't have to worry about the twins. I'll care for them."

"I know," Tom replied, "but I had an idea. The weather is warm, and I think we should all go into Nashville together. You've helped me so much. We've been more or less tied to the cabin here for months. A trip to town would be good for all of us. I promised Hester Floyd that I'd bring the babies for her to see."

Hannah looked from Tom to Hiram. Hiram spoke, "You said last night that you needed to get some dry goods and needles. So, why don't we go with Tom?"

Before Hannah had time to answer, Hiram spoke to Tom, "She's ready to start sewing baby clothes now. Guess I can't say much, though. I'm already working on a cradle."

They all three laughed together. Even Julia Anna and Margaret Emily joined in the laughter.

The trip was planned for the next day. Hiram and Hannah went on home for a night's rest.

Chapter 8

Tom's Purchase

The Hamptons, Tom, and the twins were on their way to Nashville shortly after sunup the next morning. Tom held one of the twins, and Hannah held the other. Hiram drove the team of horses.

It was a beautiful morning. Hannah and Tom admired the wild roses that bloomed all along the trail. Tom said, "When we get back home I must pick some roses for Katie's and Sally's graves." He was silent for a time, lost in thought . . . remembering, thinking, planning, dreaming. The twins seemed to sense their pa's mood, and they didn't whimper or make a sound. Hiram and Hannah were also lost in their own thoughts. The little group rode on in silence. The only sounds were those of the wagon wheels rolling along the road, the sound of the horses' hooves striking the ground, and the squirrels chattering as they moved through the tops of the trees.

Finally Tom spoke, "While you are in the area, will you place some flowers on the graves of my loved ones that I am leaving here? A spring rose, a summer daisy, an autumn aster, and perhaps even a green cedar bough at Christmastime. Sarah and Katie were both good girls . . . good women . . . good wives. I buried Sarah holding her baby, and I'll take Katie's babies with me."

He looked at the twins and said, "I'll keep the memory of your mama alive for you."

Hannah said, "You can count on me. Flowers will be on the graves of those you love."

They rode on without speaking for a time. Then Tom said, "We carry our past with us always. We must live in the present and plan for the future. And speaking of the future, let's talk about the household goods that I'll need for the long journey and for my new home in the Ozarks. Hiram and I have already sorted the blacksmith and farming tools. I know tools better than I know cooking and household stuff."

The three of them laughed, and the mood became jovial again. Tom continued speaking, "I have my Dutch oven, dinner pot, and teakettle. Katie and I had talked of our need for a big, black, iron kettle—one to use outside when needed, one that can be used for so many things . . . washing and boiling clothes, making soap, cooking corn into hominy, rendering lard at butchering time. Oh, the uses for a big iron pot are endless. I must buy one before I leave Indiana. I think I should buy one in Nashville today."

Hiram laughed and said, "As long as we are neighbors, you can always borrow ours."

"I know. I know," Tom replied. "Land of Goshen, guess your black kettle has spent as much time at my cabin as it has at yours. It's been on the road so much that it's been a kettle without a home. But now it's time, past time, for me to have my own black kettle."

"I've been thinking," Tom continued. "Thinking about what the girls will ride in. You know I never did get that second cradle made. I've decided to put the cradle that I have right behind the spring seat in the wagon. Then I'll make a box about the size of a cradle and put it in the front corner of the wagon. I'll put the black kettle in the other corner and put pillows and a quilt in it. One of the babies can ride in it part of the time."

He looked at the babies and said, "Girls, when you are asked how and when you moved to Missouri, you can say, 'I went in the summer of 1845, riding in a big, black kettle.'"

The girls laughed out loud, and their little black eyes twinkled. The three adults laughed, too. Soon they were in Nashville. Hiram drove the wagon to the Floyds' home. Tom and Hannah took the babies and went into the house.

Hester Floyd was delighted to see the twins. Tom knew that he needed to hurry . . . to get right on and meet Jackson. He was anxious to see how many families were going . . . to talk about a starting date, to plan a route. But he stayed in the Floyds' house to hear Hester talk about the twins. He beamed as she said, "Oh, they are beautiful, beautiful, beautiful! But, how can you tell them apart? They have so much black hair, and just see those black eyes twinkle. Their features are like Katie, but they have your coloring, Tom."

As Tom opened the door to leave he said,

"Hiram is waiting, and probably Jackson is, too. I'll go on and leave you women. Don't completely spoil my girls. You know when we hit the trail, it will be just me and them in the wagon for weeks and weeks and weeks. Can't have babies who want to be held all of the time."

Hannah and Hester enjoyed having the day to visit and to take care of Julia Anna and Margaret Emily. Hester expressed her happiness and surprise when Hannah told her about the baby she was expecting. Pioneer women were always busy. Their work was never done, so Hester and Hannah worked as they talked. They had a good supper ready when John, Tom, and Hiram returned to the Floyds' home just before dark. By working together they had found time to do some sewing for the twins . . . had even made each of them two new, larger dresses.

Tom was delighted when he saw the new dresses,

but he felt foolish when he discovered tears on his cheeks. He thought, "I hope that John and Hiram will understand if they see my tears . . . won't think I've become too soft-hearted . . . losing my Katie so unexpectedly . . . caring for my babies . . . watching the miracle of their growth and development . . . seeing the genuine goodness of my neighbors, the Hamptons . . . and spending so much time pondering, thinking, remembering, and planning for the future . . . the future for me and my girls. All this has changed me—a change for the better, I hope."

Tom suddenly realized that John, Hiram, Hester, and Hannah were all looking at him. "I'm sorry," he said, "I was lost in thought."

"We saw that," said Hester. "Are you ready to think about eating now?"

While they ate, they discussed the decisions that had been made that day. Tom reported that the group would start to the Ozarks on the first day of June, which would fall on a Tuesday. All of the families who planned to go together were to meet back in Nashville on the first day of June. They had agreed that the only thing which would cause them to change the date would be heavy rains or floods.

The adults talked long after the twins slept. Many different emotions were felt by the little group that night: excitement, dread, fear, happiness, and sorrow, as each of them thought of Tom's departure on such a long journey taking twin babies with him.

Early the next morning Tom, his babies, and

the Hamptons headed for home. They stopped at Brummet's Store and loaded Tom's new black kettle.

On the way home they talked of many things . . . the Floyds' hospitality and good food, plans for Tom's journey, the families who would be going with Tom, the twins and their new clothes, and the Hamptons' baby that was yet to be born. Finally Tom said, "If you aren't going to Missouri, it's time your garden was made and your corn crop planted."

Hiram said, "I know. Seems as if my heart's not been in it, though."

Tom replied, "I can see why. You've been so busy helping me. Now it's my turn. I'll help you. We'll get your seeds all planted. We'll start as soon as we get back; that is, if you'll care for the girls, Hannah."

"I want to spend as much time with Julia Anna and Margaret Emily as possible," Hannah answered. "I try not to, but sometimes I think that I will never see them again after you head to Missouri."

Tom said, "Well, life is uncertain. It's a long way to Missouri. One never knows. One never knows."

They rode the rest of the way home in silence. Each of the three occupants of the wagon was lost in thought. The twins slept peacefully.

Chapter 9

Saying Goodbye

Common sense told Tom that the days were getting longer. He knew each day had just a tad more daylight than the day before. Yet at the end of each day he found himself asking, "Where did the time go?"

He and Hiram had made a garden. Hannah did not feel well, and both Hiram and Tom felt protective of her "in her condition." Beans, pumpkin, squash, onions, and potatoes were planted. Soon the green of the young plants could be seen across the garden.

Hiram and Hannah's dog, Hanram, was kept busy keeping the deer out of the garden.

The corn crop was planted in new ground that had been prepared the previous summer and fall. The

big trees had been girdled and were now dead. They would not put out leaves this spring. The underbrush had been cut, and the small stumps and roots had been grubbed out of the ground. The corn should do well on the fertile new ground.

On the day the last seed was put into the soil, Tom said to Hiram, "Old-timers always told us to plant the corn when the oak leaves were the size of a squirrel's ears. We didn't quite make it, but with a reasonable growing season, you should have a good corn crop."

Hiram replied, "Yes, I've heard that old saying all of my life. My family said it came from the Indians."

"Probably did," Tom agreed. "Corn was their crop. Remember the stories of how the Indians taught our forefathers to plant corn."

Tom continued, "I love to hear the old stories and legends from the past. As I recall the past, I think of the future. It's only been a little over two hundred years since the white man settled this country. Not much more than fifty years since they crossed the Appalachian Mountains and settled in Kentucky, Tennessee, and on here in Indiana. And now I'm taking my girls and heading on west . . . on west to Missouri. You know Missouri is now called the 'gateway to the West.' Some even call Westport 'the jumping-off place.' I hear that many families are now going all the way to the Pacific."

Tom paused for a time, did his deep thinking, his

pondering. Then he spoke again. "The past, the present, and the future . . . wonder if any of my descendants, children and grandchildren of Julia Anna and Margaret Emily, will remember us . . . will remember and tell our stories to their descendants. What does the future hold?"

Hiram laughed and said, "Tom, the things you think about often surprise me."

Tom's loud laugh surprised Hiram, too. "Sometimes I surprise myself," he said. "I've always had a habit of pondering on things. Pondering, thinking, dreaming, and remembering."

"I observe that often," Hiram replied.

"The babies and I will be on our way to the West in a few more days. You and Hannah and how you've helped me . . . how Hannah has cared for the babies . . . all these memories will be there for me to ponder in the years to come."

Tom was silent for a time. His piercing black eyes seemed to be looking into the future. He laughed again and said, "Even old Hanram will be a memory. Imagine my telling about your old dog in Missouri . . . explaining his name. 'Han' from Han-nah and 'Ram' from Hi-ram. What a name. What a dog. And what memories to ponder in the years to come!"

The last days of May arrived. Neighbors in the sparsely settled area planned to meet at Shiloh Church the last Sunday in May. Tom was to preach the sermon, and there would be dinner on the ground. The afternoon would be spent singing, visiting, and saying goodbyes.

On Friday and Saturday Tom and Hiram loaded the wagon. Tom said, "I must take all of my main blacksmith tools with me."

He knew that the Ozark Highland region was opening up to settlement. Farmers were moving in. He would farm some, but the area would need a blacksmith shop and a good smithy. Explorers had been through the area about twenty-five years before. Hunters and trappers had taken from the streams and hills. Now the area was ready for real settlers—settlers with families who would build communities, towns, churches, and schools.

Tom knew that he would have to travel to Springfield, a distance of fifty or sixty miles from where he would be settling, to file land claims or to purchase government land. A federal land office had opened there in 1834.

Settlement was slow because the forested hills were difficult to travel through. The land was rocky and not as good for growing crops as the other areas in Missouri. By 1837 enough settlers had moved into the area to warrant the formation of Taney County. In 1841 both Ozark and Wright Counties were organized.

Tom knew that the Davis and Todd families lived in Ozark County. That was where he would head . . . where he would take the twins to be near their grandmother.

As Tom loaded his blacksmith tools, he planned and sorted carefully. He could not overload the wagon. His anvil went into the wagon first. A smithy must have his anvil! Next he loaded his hammers, tongs, post drill, and vise. He told Hiram, "When I get to the Ozarks I will build a forge out of rocks and bellows from deer hides, but I must take these tools."

After the tools were loaded so that their weight was evenly distributed, Tom said, "Now for the supplies. I must have some bar iron from which to form shoes for horses and oxen. I will also take along a little scrap iron and the horseshoe nails that I have made. Some of these will probably be needed before we complete our trip. The charcoal that I made out of green hickory makes a hot fire. I'll take some of it."

Hiram spoke, "Looks like you have planned well for the trip. You've also thought of your future shop that you will build in Missouri."

Tom said, "Bless Hannah's heart. She has already packed the few household goods that I will take along. Katie's clock and her quilts must go. The iron cooking pots are ready. Monday morning I'll load them, my axe, gun, and Bible. I have plenty of potatoes, bacon, and cured meat. I also have some dried fruit, cornmeal, beans, and rice. I'm sure we will hunt and fish some as we go along—probably kill a deer or two on the way."

Hiram said, "Hannah and I will help you finish loading on Monday morning . . . a bittersweet day."

"Yes," Tom agreed. "Yes."

It was evening by the time the tools were loaded into the wagon. Tom inspected the harness one more time. Then he checked the drawstrings in the canvas at the front and back of the wagon. He wanted to make sure the ends of the wagon could be closed. His girls must be kept snug and dry. He also checked to see that the sides of the canvas could be rolled up. In July and August they would need the breeze to blow through the wagon. He was satisfied with the final inspection. The wagon was ready to be moved to the cabin. Monday morning they would load the cradle, the household goods, and the food.

Tom spoke to Hiram. "If you don't mind, go on into the cabin and tell Hannah that I will be in shortly. I want to walk up on the hill . . . visit the graves just one more time." On the way he picked a couple of wild roses, one for each grave.

Hannah had supper ready when Tom got back to the cabin. He walked to the bed and picked up both babies. Silently he stood holding them. At last he spoke. "It's been a long six months. I pray that I've made the right decision." Again the occupants of the little cabin were silent . . . each of them lost in thought.

Hannah said, "Let's eat the stew and corn pone, and then we'll talk about tomorrow. I've already fed Julia Anna and Margaret Emily."

While they ate, Hannah told Tom and Hiram about what she had cooked to take to church for dinner

the next day. Tom said, "It all sounds good, and I may eat all of the dried-apple pie myself. Don't imagine that I'll have a chance to eat pie again for some time. Ah, but I'll have the memory of your good dried-apple pies! Memories to ponder. Memories which will make my mouth water."

Hiram and Hannah laughed. They agreed they would all go to church in Hiram's wagon since Tom's wagon was already covered and loaded. Hiram and Hannah went to their cabin for the night.

Early the next morning the Hamptons returned to Tom's cabin. Hannah helped Tom bathe the twins and dress them in one of their new dresses. Then she combed their black hair into a curl on top of their heads. Their little black eyes twinkled, and they each ooed and gooed with happiness. The sound of their laughter filled the little cabin. Tom said, "I don't want to spoil them or see them become vain . . . but, oh, don't they look pretty!"

Hiram laughed, "Two peas in a pod. Suppose they will always look so much alike?"

The dinner, packed in a wooden box, was loaded into the wagon. Tom picked up his well-worn Bible and his hymn book in one arm and Margaret Emily in the other one. Hannah picked up Julia Anna. They loaded into the wagon and were off to church.

When they arrived at the church house, Tom was surprised to see that almost everyone in the area was there.

The singing was spirited. What Tom, Hiram, and the others lacked in musical ability, they made up for in volume. A time of testifying, of sharing the goodness of God, followed the singing. Then Tom began preaching. He spoke of neighbors . . . of the lawyer asking Jesus, "And who is my neighbor?" He retold the parable of the

good Samaritan. He reminisced . . . told of "good Samaritans" that he had encountered in Brown County. He recalled the building of the log church in which they were worshiping and spoke of those who had already made the "great journey." When he finished his sermon with, "God be with us all till we meet again," there were few dry eyes in the little log building.

After eating a bountiful dinner, the little group spent the afternoon singing and visiting. Each woman and young girl took turns holding Julia Anna and Margaret Emily. The twins, although a little less than six months old, knew they were the center of attention. Their bright little black eyes took in everything.

Finally the last goodbyes were said, and the families went on their way to their own homes.

On the ride home Tom, Hiram, and Hannah were all quiet. The girls slept.

When they reached Tom's cabin, Hannah said, "Tom, I'll leave you some food, and we'll go on home." Tom understood. He knew that Hannah was tired and emotionally spent.

He and Hiram carried the babies into the cabin, and Hiram and Hannah went on home. Hiram said, "See you early in the morning."

Tom sat in the cabin throughout that evening. He sat there with his babies, knowing this was the last night he would spend in the little log cabin that had been his home for over five years. He pondered and remembered many things . . . good times and bad times. Both happy and sad thoughts flashed through his mind.

He heard the twins stirring. He picked them up . . . held them both . . . held them and sang to them.

We're headin' west tomorrow.
　　Can't you hear the wagons creak?
We'll cross the Mississippi
　　Though it's mighty wide and deep.
The sky will be our ceiling,
　　And under the stars we'll sleep,
But we'll keep on moving westward
　　For weeks and weeks and weeks.
The journey won't be easy,
　　But I'll be there all the way.
God in Heaven, do go with us,
　　And keep us safe, I pray.

Chapter 10

On the Road

Monday morning's weather was almost perfect: warm, but not too hot. A gentle breeze blew, but it was not windy. A few lazy clouds floated in the sky, but it did not look rainy. The shape of one fluffy, white cloud made Tom think of an angel's wings. He thought, "I hope that is a good-luck omen. I've never been superstitious, but it would be comforting to think of a guardian angel hovering over my babies as we make this long, hard trip."

Tom's emotions fit the weather. He was almost totally at peace with himself and his decision. Yet a few clouds of fear . . . a few "what ifs" . . . crept into his thoughts. He knew that Hiram and Hannah would be at the cabin shortly. He thought, "I must be positive in all I say and do. I cannot let these good friends of mine see that I have even a shadow of doubt or fear."

Silently he prayed, "God in Heaven, take care of Hannah and her baby. Let her bring a live baby into this world. Let her live to care for it."

After losing both Sally and Katie, the fear of childbirth would be with Tom forever.

Hiram and Hannah had discussed having to tell Tom and the twins goodbye. They knew it would not be easy. Hannah said, "I will try to keep from crying. If I have to cry, I hope Tom will understand, will not think that we object to their going. But, oh, it will be so hard to tell Julia Anna and Margaret Emily goodbye. Maybe for the last time . . ."

"Now, now," interrupted Hiram. "You know a wagon train of people head west each spring. Many of them are on their way to Missouri. We may go next summer. After the baby . . . if all goes well, we may join Tom and the twins."

"More roads are being built at this time. Soon it should be easier to send letters. Tom will keep in touch. He won't just move off and forget us," Hannah added.

The bark of Tom's hound dog announced the Hamptons' arrival. Tom opened the door and said, "Come in, come in, come in." He was determined to keep this final hour with his friends as cheerful as possible.

Hannah went immediately to Julia Anna and Margaret Emily. It was obvious that both of the babies were happy to see her. Their black eyes twinkled, and they laughed as she talked to them. "Oh, girls," she said, "I've enjoyed you so much!"

The baby that she was carrying chose that moment to kick and to change position. She placed her hand on her stomach and said, "I still find it hard to believe: I'm going to be a real mother at last. But I'll miss you girls. You'll both always have a special place in my heart."

She then took two little pink bonnets out of the basket that she had carried in with her. She put one on each baby and tied the strings under their chins. The bonnets were made out of the pink calico that was left from the new dresses that she and Hester Floyd had made for the twins. She said, "You both look pretty. Your pa needs to keep a bonnet on you. We don't want your soft, fair, baby skin getting all tanned from the sun and wind."

Before Hannah had finished speaking, Julia Anna had managed to get her new bonnet untied. Off it came, and her expression showed her feelings about wearing a bonnet.

"So much for that plan," Hannah laughed.

Tom and Hiram harnessed the four workhorses and hitched them to the wagon. The young cow that would continue to furnish the milk for the twins was tied to the back of the wagon. Dan, Tom's beautiful bay saddle horse, was also tied to the wagon.

Brownie, Tom's old hound, was darting under the wagon and out again. He circled the cabin and the blacksmith shop. Then he was back at the wagon for another inspection of it. Finally he threw back his head and howled. It seemed as if he were saying, "I've checked everything. Looks to me like we are ready to be on our way. Who knows what adventures lie between here and the wilds of Missouri's Ozarks?"

Tom and Hiram went into the cabin. Hiram picked up Julia Anna, and Tom picked up Margaret Emily. Hannah folded the last of the quilts and the bedding. The wagon was full, so the bed would not be taken. Tom would build a new bed when he needed one in Missouri. Tom handed Margaret Emily to Hannah. He picked up the folded bedding and loaded it into the wagon.

The girls ooed and gooed and laughed, but the three adults said nothing.

Tom came back into the almost-empty cabin. He looked around for the last time. He was glad that they were not talking . . . glad that Hannah and Hiram would not have to hear his voice quivering. He looked at his friends. Each of them was holding one of his babies. He turned his back and went out the cabin door. Hiram and Hannah followed him. Tom paused and closed the cabin door, leaving the latchstring loose and free on the outside. He put one arm around Hannah's shoulders and a hand on Hiram's elbow. The three of them walked silently to the wagon.

Hannah kissed Margaret Emily on each cheek and handed her to Tom. He placed her in the cradle that was just behind the wagon seat. Hiram handed Julia Anna to Hannah, and she kissed her cheeks. Then she handed the second baby to Tom, and he put her into the cradle beside Margaret Emily.

Hiram looked at the twins and then at Hannah. He put his arm around her. Tom stepped toward his friends . . . stood in front of them. All three of them looked at each other, each lost in emotions too deep to express with words. Finally Hiram said, "May God go with you and the babies every mile and every day of this journey." Hannah did not trust herself to speak.

Tom said, "Friends, I'll never forget you. I will pray for you each day. You know . . ."

"Yes, we do know. We know each other so well that we don't need to say any more," Hiram replied.

Tom climbed onto the wagon seat, picked up the lines, and said, "Get up, Bill. Get up, Ribbon. Let's go, Bess and Bird." The covered wagon rolled forward, heading toward Nashville.

Hannah and Hiram stood as if rooted to the spot, stood looking at the wagon until it was lost from sight, stood looking into the distance until it seemed that the trees had swallowed the wagon and its occupants.

71

When Hannah could no longer see a sign of the wagon, she stopped waving. She picked up the edges of her apron and covered her face. Then she let her tears flow freely. Hiram put his arm around her, but neither of them spoke.

Finally they turned and headed toward their own cabin. When they entered it, they sensed a different feeling . . . more lonely . . . more isolated. Not having neighbors, good neighbors, just over the hill would be difficult.

Hiram said, "I think I'll work on the cradle. Smooth and polish more on the walnut wood that I'm making it out of. I found a piece of broken glass that is just right for a scrapper. With a little more work, I can have that wood as smooth as glass."

Hannah said, "I wish you would stay around the cabin. I feel the need of your nearness. I'm going to work on weaving a blanket out of that soft thread that I spun. I got just the right amount of indigo when I dyed it. It's the perfect color for a baby . . . blue as the sky."

"Reminded me of a robin's egg," Hiram said. "Let's get to work. Get on with our lives. Just think, our own baby will be here in another four months . . . early October. It will need a warm coverlet and a cradle by the fireplace."

Hannah said, "If it's a boy let's name him Thomas Hiram . . . Thomas Hiram Hampton."

"A girl could be called Emily Anna . . . Emily Anna Hampton," Hiram added.

Hannah continued, "Or twins . . . "

"Oh, no!" Hiram exclaimed. They laughed and were ready to go on with their lives, their future in Brown County.

When Tom left his cabin, he never looked back. He spoke to the girls. "Our faces will face the setting sun for weeks now. As we load up the wagon and head out in the mornings, the sun will be behind us, over our shoulders, and all afternoon we will follow the setting sun. Follow it for over five hundred miles. All the way to the Ozarks."

The happy baby noises and the sound of his own voice comforted Tom. He continued talking to the twins. "When we get to Nashville, I'll take you to Hester's home and leave you for the rest of the day. Then I'll meet the Fleetwoods, John Hopper, and Squire Rippee's family. We'll go over the wagons and check our supplies again. The other families going with us are using oxen to pull their wagons. May be smarter with the roads as they are. By using horses, though, I can spend more time in the wagon with you girls. I'll get some oxen when we get to the Ozarks. I would rather have horses for the trip. And we should be ready to pull out early in the morning."

Tom did not talk for a time. He turned his head and looked at the babies. Both of them were sound asleep with their heads on the same pillow. Tom drove the rest of the way in silence. His next words were, "Whoa, Bill. Whoa, Ribbon. Whoa, Bess and Bird."

The horses stopped in front of the Floyds' home, and the twins woke up.

Chapter 11

Goodbye to Nashville

John Floyd helped Hester catch and kill a fat hen before he left the house. "Chicken and dumplings are Tom's favorite!" she said. "I'll also have new peas and potatoes. Tom loves to eat. And this last supper at our house must be one he will remember." The words "last supper" caused Hester to catch her breath. She gave way to her feelings of fear, dread, and worry and cried softly.

"Such a long, hard journey for a man, but oh, a man taking along two babies. Can he make it, John? All that way! What if . . ."

"Now, now," John interrupted. "You know that Tom had always been sensible and hard working. He won't take any unnecessary chances. He's doing what he feels he must do . . . what he feels is best for his babies. We must show him our support."

"I will. I will. I'll not let him see my tears, but I'm so worried."

Hester kept herself busy in her kitchen all morning. She made both dried-peach and dried-apple fried pies. She thought, "There'll be plenty of these left over. I'll tuck a goodly number of them into Tom's grub box before he pulls out in the morning."

Hester kept an alert ear as she worked, and she heard Tom's wagon coming. By the time he had said,

"Whoa," to his horses, Hester was reaching her arms up for a baby. She could not help thinking of herself as "Grandma," although she knew that she was no blood kin to the twins. She found herself thinking, "If only my daughter, Sarah, and her baby could have lived . . ." Lost in thought she said, "Hand one of those precious little babies to Granny." She took the baby Tom handed her and added, "Now, tell me, which one do I have?"

"Granny, you are holding Margaret Emily. I'm going to have to come up with some way for people to tell my girls apart," Tom said as he picked up Julia Anna and climbed out of the wagon.

Both adults said nothing as they headed toward the house, each of them carrying a baby. Tom was lost in his pondering, thinking, and remembering. He thought of the death of Sally and her baby, Hester's daughter, and the grandchild that she had wanted so badly. He hugged Julia Anna a little closer and thought, "Oh, Hester, I know that you still feel the pain of your loss. It will be hard to say goodbye to you and John in the morning. You have been like parents to me."

Hester, too, was thinking of Sally and the baby that was buried with her. "We have our memories. We don't really lose those who go away from us . . . either by death or by distance."

"Yes," Tom agreed. "We cannot stop the hands of time. Life can and must go on."

Tom and Hester entered the house, and Hester

said, "I've made a pallet on the kitchen floor. We'll put the twins in there."

"Doesn't look like that is all you've made," Tom said, eyeing the pot of chicken and the spicy-smelling fried pies.

They put the twins on the pallet Hester had prepared. She gave Tom a bowl of chicken and dumplings and one of each kind of the fried pies. "Maybe this will hold you until supper."

Tom ate and told Hester that he would go on down to Brummet's Store. He planned to meet Jackson and the other men who would be joining their wagon train to the Missouri Ozarks.

He walked to the pallet to tell Julia Anna and Margaret Emily goodbye. They were busy playing with two new soft rag dolls that Hester had made for them. Tom said, "Well, well, girls. Kind of hard for your old pa to admit to himself that your affection has turned to a rag doll and left him out." He laughed and turned to Hester. "See you by supper time. I won't be late."

When he got to Brummet's Store, he found Jackson waiting. Squire Rippee and John Hopper were with him. They reported that their wagons were loaded, and their families were ready to start. They were all camped together at a spring on the north side of Nashville.

Tom said, "My wagon is ready. It's in front of John Floyd's house. I'll be at camp and ready to roll in the morning.   My girls are with Hester Floyd now. They are ready to go."

John Hopper said, "Tom, Martha is eager to help watch the twins on the trip."

Jackson said, "All of the women are ready to help you with the babies, Tom.   My two big girls, Abigail and Elizabeth, have been fighting over which one of them can help.   I finally said, 'Hush, girls. They're twins, so each of you can have one.'   Just wait until your girls are big enough to fight, Tom."

Tom replied, "Well, I won't worry about that for a while.   Sounds like I'll have plenty of help with my babies."

The men continued talking as they walked on toward the camp where the wagons were parked.   Tom wanted to inspect the wagons with his trained "black-smith's eyes," wanted to see if he thought they were road ready for the long trip.

As they walked along, Tom said, "I am bringing along my tools, and I'm sure each of you has an ample supply of axle grease as well as all your other supplies."

Jackson laughed and said, "I told the men that you would check the wagons over carefully.   We've all agreed that we will look to you as our leader.   Guess you could say that you've been chosen, or elected, our wagon master.   That is, if you will accept the job."

Tom replied, "I'll do my part . . . do all I can to be of help to any of you.   We'll have to work together if we are to successfully complete this journey.   I'll have to admit that I've had some doubts . . . even fears. Yes, yes, we must all work together!"

When they arrived at camp, Tom wanted to meet all of the children. They all rushed out to greet the men. Several of them said together, "If Mr. Brown is here, can we start? Can we start? Are we ready to start now?"

Jackson said, "Tom, this here's my Abigail and Elizabeth. Here's Isaac, my oldest. He's twelve and will be a big help. And this here's Joseph."

Joseph hastily added, "And I'm five going on six. I'll be six on July 4. And this is my dog, Ring."

Tom looked at the Fleetwood family. Jackson's wife, Mahala, was a pleasant but serious-looking woman. The older three children were quiet and well mannered. Little Joseph's eyes, almost hidden by a mop of unruly black hair, danced with mischief. Tom thought, "If I'm not mistaken, that young man will make things interesting."

Squire Rippee was about Tom's age, early thirties. He said, "Tom, you've not met my woman. Took me a long time to find one who would have me. But Matilda finally said, 'Yes,' and we tied the knot in May. When her ma found out that we'd be moving so far away, all the way to Missouri, she tried to talk her out of marryin' me. This here is Matilda."

"Hello, Mr. Brown," said Matilda.

"Now none of that Mr. Brown stuff. I'm Tom."

"I'm anxious to see your twins. I love babies.

But then everybody loves babies, don't they?" Matilda replied shyly.

Next John Hopper said, "Well, Tom, here's my family. Wife, Martha, and baby, Johnnie. Nathaniel, Elizabeth, George Washington, and Mary Ann. Mary Ann is eight now, almost nine, and the others all come two years apart. Martha and I have been married ten years and have five kids. If we keep havin' one every other year, we could have a passel of 'em by the time that I'm fifty."

"Oh, John, hush your foolishness," Martha demanded. Tom could see by the twinkle in her eyes that she enjoyed John's "foolishness."

By the time the final introductions had been made, Abigail Jackson had informed the other children that she would not be playing with them on the trip. She said, "I will be helping care for the Brown twins: two little girls, Margaret Emily and Julia Anna. My sister, Elizabeth, will help me."

The oldest Hopper girl, Mary Ann, had always helped care for her younger brothers and sisters. She said, "So what? Who cares?" But even she was excited about the twins.

Tom did look the three wagons over carefully. He was pleased with what he saw. He and the men sat down on the ground by the spring. Each of them leaned back against a tree. They discussed the route they would be taking toward the west.

Tom was satisfied that they all had planned well.

They were as prepared as they could be. After the men had discussed everything that needed to be discussed, Tom said, "I must get back to the Floyds' home. I will be here with my wagon by seven o'clock in the morning. I'll be ready to start the journey toward the west."

Chapter 12

Wagons West

John and Tom arrived back at the Floyds' home at the same time. Hester was sitting on a pallet on the kitchen floor playing with Julia Anna and Margaret Emily. She was singing a funny little song with actions, and both babies were watching each move that she made. They were laughing and moving their little hands and arms in various gestures. Hester was so fascinated watching the twins that she did not hear John and Tom come into the kitchen. John said, "Well, well, Granny, you're down on the floor, but can you get up?"

"Watch your tongue, old man. You're older than I am." They all laughed. It seemed that Julia Anna and Margaret Emily understood the humor. They both laughed.

Hester said, "I'll tell you before you ask. Supper is ready. The twins and old Brownie have already been fed. Tom, that old dog can almost talk. He whimpered and howled so pitifully when you left, like he thought he was being left behind. I finally called him up to the kitchen door. When he saw the babies, he lay down and hasn't made another sound. His actions said, 'Tom wouldn't leave those babies behind for long, so I know that he will be back for me.'"

Tom said, "He's a hound, so hunting is in his blood, but he sure is protective of the babies."

"Let's wash up," John said. "Hester had me out chasing that chicken before breakfast. Let's see if it was worth the trouble."

Hester dished up the food while the men washed for supper. They sat down, and John said, "Tom, ask the blessing." Tom prayed. The three of them talked little as they ate.

After they ate Tom and John went out to the barn to check on the horses. Hester cleared the table and did the dishes.

Julia Anna and Margaret Emily had not taken an afternoon nap. Hester saw that they were sleepy, so she put them to bed. She kissed each of them good night and said aloud, "Precious, precious little girls. May God go with you and your pa."

John and Tom came back into the house, and the three of them talked for a while. They found the conversation was about the past instead of the present or the future.

Hester finally asked, "Tom, what did you think of Squire Rippee's new wife, Matilda?"

"She's young, but she seemed sensible and caring. She assured me that she would help with the babies. Mahala will also help. Her girls, they are nine and ten now, they want to help, too."

"I saw young Isaac Fleetwood the other day. That boy is almost grown. Going to be as big as his pa soon," John added.

Tom told Hester and John that he had arranged to eat most of his meals with the Fleetwoods. "Mahala is a good cook, and sometimes I have trouble boiling water. I can't imagine trying to cook on a campfire and doing all the things that I'll need to be doing." He hastily added, "I'm taking along plenty of food. We will use it, but I won't object to letting Mahala cook it."

John said, "In a way, I wish Hester and I were going with you."

Hester hastily added, "No, no. We're too old to transplant, but you'll always know where to find us, Tom."

Tom replied, "Well, there will be eighteen of us making the journey. That's counting the twins and John and Martha Hopper's baby, Johnnie. And speaking of the journey, I need to be up early in the morning. This will be my last night in a real bed for a long time. Do you mind if I turn in now?"

Hester said, "Your bed is ready. It's time for all of us to be in bed." So, the three of them went on to bed. None of them slept much. Their heads and hearts were too full of memories and emotions. Hester was up shortly after four the next morning. Both Tom and John heard her when she went into the kitchen to build the fire. They got up soon after she did.

While Hester cooked breakfast, Tom milked the cow so the twins would have their breakfast. He carefully checked over his wagon and its load and the horses and their harness. All was in readiness, he decided.

By the time Tom got back into the house, Hester had already dressed Julia Anna and Margaret Emily. She and Tom fed them their breakfast of warm, fresh milk and the oatmeal which Hester had cooked. Tom looked at them and said, "You are two little early birds, for sure. History will tell about pioneer fathers and mothers, but you two will be pioneer twin babies. You will be part of that history, too."

Hester said, "Breakfast is ready. John and I don't eat much this early in the morning. We'll sit at the table with you, and each of us will hold one of the babies while you eat, Tom."

Tom understood. He sat down and ate. John held Julia Anna while Hester held Margaret Emily. The clock ticked the minutes away. The goodbyes had to be said.

Tom arrived at camp shortly after six. He was surprised to see that breakfast was over, and the three wagons and their occupants were all ready to be on the road. He smiled to himself and thought, "Wonder if we'll be this eager to be on the trail in a couple of months?"

The little group greeted Tom. Before he was out of his wagon, the Fleetwood girls, Abigail and Elizabeth, were saying, "Can we ride with you and the twins? Can we please?

"It's fine with me, girls, but we'll need to ask your ma."

Jackson said, "Girls, get away and quit bothering Tom before we're even on the road."

Squire Rippee and John Hopper approached Tom's wagon. "You're early, Tom," Squire said.

"But, we're all ready to roll toward the west, to Missouri," John hastily added.

"Good morning, ladies and children. Hello there, Isaac." Tom knew that he must not address Isaac as one of the children.

"Good morning, Uncle Tom. The girls and I decided to call you Uncle Tom instead of Mr. Brown. Ma said that would be respectful. You don't mind, do you?"

"Makes me feel good, Isaac. We are four families. The Fleetwoods, Rippees, Hoppers, and Browns, but we must work with each other, be all like one big family, if we are to complete this long journey successfully."

"Right. Right," chorused the others in the group.

"Tom, you go ahead and lead off when you are ready. Our other wagons will follow you. Your horses could be faster than the oxen that are pulling the other three wagons. We know that you won't push your horses, and we all have good young oxen which are well trained."

Tom replied, "Slow but steady should be our pace, I think." He climbed up in his wagon where Abigail and Elizabeth were already seated.

Tom picked up the reins and said, "Get up. Let's go, Bill and Ribbon. Get up, Bess and Bird. We're off to the Missouri Ozarks on Tuesday, the second day of

June, 1845." He spoke to the Fleetwood sisters. "You girls are old enough to remember this journey. Remember it, and tell your children and your grandchildren about it. My twins will not remember this trip, this year, but I will remember. I will remember and tell them."

After a time Tom looked back. Three wagons were in line behind him. The women and children rode on seats near the front of the wagon. Squire, Jackson, and John each carried a goad and walked beside their lead ox.

They were leaving Nashville behind them and heading toward Indianapolis. At Indianapolis they would get on the road that headed west—west and a little south toward St. Louis. Tom had heard of the new-fangled steam-powered ferries which were there. He was eager to see the Mississippi, that great river that split the country into the "East" and the "West"; eager to see a city as large and old as St. Louis; eager to see how the use of steam for power could push a boat; eager and excited . . . and yet a little fearful and apprehensive.

Chapter 13

The Mississippi Behind Us

Nashville was about sixty miles south of Indianapolis. The first five days of travel were pleasant. The men thought they made good time as they covered twelve or thirteen miles each day. On Saturday night they made camp near a spring on the south edge of Indianapolis.

Tom was concerned about both babies. They had fretted and cried much of the day. He did not seem to be able to pacify them. As soon as the wagons stopped, Tom went to the Fleetwoods' wagon. "Mahala, I'm concerned about the babies. Fussing like they have today is not like them. I wonder if you would . . ."

Before Tom could finish speaking, Mahala was at his wagon. She had Julia Anna in one arm and Margaret Emily in the other. "Now, now, girls, your pa says that you are both fussy. Let's see if we can find out why." Before she even laid the babies down she saw that the fronts of their dresses were wet from their drooling. She put the twins on the old quilt that Tom used for a pallet on the ground. Then she told Abigail and Elizabeth to watch them for a minute.

Isaac said, "Uncle Tom, I'll unhitch your team and water them."

"Bless you, Isaac, you are such a help to all of us."

Mahala had gone to the spring and washed her hands carefully. She took some of the cold spring water and went back to the twins. She opened Julia Anna's mouth and rubbed her gums. Then she checked Margaret Emily's gums. "Just as I thought, Tom. Your babies are teething. Not really sick, but they'll be fussy for a few days." She continued to dip her forefinger into the water and rub the twins' gums. The cool water was soothing, and soon both babies were asleep. Tom drew a sigh of relief.

The little group had settled into a routine. When the wagons stopped, the men cared for the stock and checked over the wagons. Matilda, Squire's young wife, helped the older girls, Abigail and Elizabeth Fleetwood and Mary Ann Hopper, gather wood enough to cook the meals for all of them for that night and the next morning. Isaac carried water. Martha Hopper and Mahala Fleetwood cared for the twins and the two young Hoppers and started the evening meals. A spirit of cooperation could be felt by everyone. Even the weather was cooperating. The temperature was pleasant for June, and there had been no rain.

Tom spoke to the group. "Friends, I am against traveling on Sunday. The Lord set that day aside for a day of rest. I think we should follow His teachings."

"The stock, the kids, and all of us need it . . . will need it even more as the weeks turn into months," Tom continued. "I can't believe that we'll gain anything by traveling on Sunday."

Martha Hopper seemed hesitant, but spoke. "By next Saturday we'll need to stop early and wash our clothes."

"And do our house cleaning. I mean wagon cleaning," Martha Rippee said, laughing.

"Yeah, yeah," grumbled Jackson. "Between Tom's preachin'—and I imagine you'll find someone to preach to on Sundays, Tom—and you women fussin' about washin' and cleanin', we may not make it to the Ozarks by frost."

"Now, Jackson," said Mahala. But Jackson had grabbed his gun and left the group. His keen, black eyes had spotted three deer in the distance. He yelled back over his shoulder, "Don't wait supper for me. We could have fresh meat for Sunday dinner . . . after the preaching, that is, Tom."

It was two hundred and fifty miles from Indianapolis to St. Louis. Roads were little more than blazed trails in some places. Still the little group forged westward at a steady pace.

Joseph Fleetwood's sixth birthday was July fourth. Tom said, "Your birthday and the birthday of our country."

"Huh?" said Joseph, not really understanding. Even if he had understood, Joseph was far more interested in his own special day than he was in hearing about the birthday of a country.

Since the fourth fell on a Saturday, the group had made camp early. Mahala used the Dutch oven in the coals of the campfire and baked Joseph a birthday cake.

Tom had deer hides in his wagon. He planned to use them to make the bellows for his new blacksmith shop. "I'll make that young man a bow and arrow," Tom thought. He cut a narrow strip of leather from one of the hides. Then he found a green hickory sprout which was just the right size. Using his pocketknife, which was always sharp, Tom trimmed the stick and bent and notched it. He made a fine bow for Joseph. Then he used a little more of the leather from the deer hides and put together a quiver for him. Isaac helped Tom, and they filled the quiver with arrows.

Mahala had been working on a shirt for Joseph. She gave it to him after they had eaten the birthday cake. He put it on and said, "Buckskin! Just like a real Indian boy would wear."

Tom handed him the bow and arrow and the quiver with the extra arrows. "Guess this is for you, too. It's too small for Isaac to use, and none of the girls would want it."

"Oh, Uncle Tom, can I go hunting with it? Right now? Tonight? Do you think that we will see an Indian

before we get to the Ozarks? Do you? Can I try it out now?"

"Settle down, boy. Calm down, or you'll scare every animal clean out of Illinois," Jackson said to his son. "Go on. Try it out."

"Don't go far from camp," Mahala added.

"I'll keep an eye on him," Isaac said. And the two brothers walked toward the woods.

Tom walked over to the pallet where both of his babies sat. He picked them up. Both babies laughed and showed their new front teeth. Their little black eyes twinkled and danced. Their skin was tanned to a soft, beautiful shade of olive. Tom smiled as he remembered the sunbonnets that Hannah had made for them. He said, "Girls, I wish Hannah could see you now. She worried about your baby-soft skin tanning. It has tanned for sure. But I believe that even Hannah would agree that it just makes you look prettier . . . makes your black hair and eyes look even blacker. Your new little teeth are like pearls. Oh, how I wish your mama could see you!"

Margaret Emily and Julia Anna laughed and looked at each other. It seemed they were developing their own special way of communicating.

Day after day went by. The group kept on following the setting sun. By mid-July they had reached the Mississippi River. Tom and the other men could not believe how black and fertile the river soil appeared to be. Each person in the little group was amazed at the size of the Mississippi River. No one in the group had seen a steamboat before. Their feelings were mixed. They ranged from fear and apprehension to awe and amazement. Just across the great river lay the city of St. Louis. Tom had heard that almost twenty thousand people lived there. He spoke to the adults in the group. "We've never seen anything like this before. There's a lot to see . . . a lot to think about. There's one thing that I feel certain about, though. This would not be a place that I would want to settle . . . not a place that I would want to raise my girls."

The three women in the little group answered together. "Right. Right."

Even Jackson joined in. "You'd have to travel for miles to find any good hunting. I wonder if the fish from such a big, muddy river would be fit to eat. And you'd probably never see another bear!"

Tom said, "Let's put it behind us as fast as we can and plow on toward the Ozarks, to a place like we are used to."

"Where you can still hunt deer and turkey and maybe even a bear," interrupted Jackson.

"And maybe even see an Indian?" inquired Joseph, who had his bow and arrow in his hand. His quiver of arrows was slung over his shoulder.

The next day the little group, three wagons each of them pulled by four oxen and Tom's wagon pulled by his faithful horses, crossed the mighty Mississippi River. They crossed on a steam-powered ferry boat.

The cow that continued to supply milk for Julia Anna and Margaret Emily was still securely tied behind Tom's wagon. Tom's old hound, Brownie, stayed right under the wagon. His mournful howl seemed to say, "Oh, I wish that we were all safely back in old Brown County."

Tom spoke to himself or maybe to his twins. "Oh, I wish we were safely settled in the Ozarks. We are a little over half of the way now. Thank the Lord, there are no more rivers to cross, not like the Mississippi, at least. No more rivers to cross!"

Tom's smile showed his sense of relief. A feeling of thankfulness filled him. The great Mississippi River was behind them. They were on Missouri soil. His girls were healthy and traveling well.

The little group camped for the night. They agreed that they were happy to leave the city of St. Louis behind them.

The roads across Indiana and Illinois were not good, but in Missouri they were worse. "At least we are on Missouri soil," Tom said.

"And traveling on trails left by the Indians," Jackson grumbled.

Tom laughed, "You're probably right, Jackson."

The group headed southwest from St. Louis toward Rolla. It was hard to cover many miles in a day. Tom knew that Springfield was farther north and west than they wanted to go. At Marshfield they headed southeast toward Ozark County.

Jackson didn't think it was possible, but the roads got worse. Tom said, "We have had little rain, so we aren't traveling through mud. We all have axes and know how to use them if we have to clear a way. We will make it to the Ozarks in spite of the roads. Many others have. Some of them from right where we started in Indiana."

"I wonder if they rode in on goats," Jackson replied.

"Oh, Jackson, you'd complain if they were goin' to hang you with a new piece of rope," John Hopper said laughingly.

They all laughed. Hardships were easier to endure when mixed with good humor. They had been on the road for almost three months, but they were near the end of their journey.

Chapter 14

A Family Reunion

During the first week of September the little group from Indiana arrived in Ozark County. This was the area where they all planned to settle.

The Fleetwoods had relatives from Indiana who had come to the Ozarks a few years earlier. Jackson planned to go to them . . . see what advice they had for him. Families helped each other. Jackson and Mahala knew that Uncle Adam and Uncle Isaac and their families would be anxious to see them and to hear news from Indiana. So before the little group crossed Bryant Creek, Jackson and his family said goodbye to the others and went on their own way.

Abigail and Elizabeth both cried when it was time to say goodbye to Julia Anna and Margaret Emily. Tom said, "Girls, you've been a big help in watching the twins. I'll bring them to see you. I promise."

Squire Rippee and his young wife, Matilda, stopped near a clear stream. They chose a beautiful spot for a home place near that stream. They soon discovered that the creek had not been given a name. Squire said, "Well, it's Rippee Creek now." Matilda was very anxious for them to get settled and to start their own cabin. She knew that there would be a baby in their home before the winter was over.

The Hoppers found a likely spot near a big spring where they decided to settle. There were neighbors who would help them get a cabin built. Time must not be wasted if John was to have a cabin ready for Martha and his five young ones before cold weather was upon them.

Tom felt a sense of loneliness at the breaking up of the little group who had spent the last three months together. They had lived as one big family, had worked together, eaten together, laughed together, and prayed together. He knew that they would always have a special feeling for each other. They would each go their separate ways, but they would never forget their trip to the Ozarks. Tom said to himself, "More to ponder, think about, and remember, if I ever have time for my pondering again." He was eager to get on with his own plans. His team was headed toward Fox Creek, where he knew the Davis family lived. Catherine would be so happy to see her granddaughters.

Tom talked to the twins as they rode along. They were a little over eight months old now. Their little black eyes took in everything around them.

Before dark Brownie ran on in front of the wagon, where he was met by another hound dog about his size. Tom exclaimed, "Brownie, get back here and hush. You've seen a hound before. We're on the last leg of the trip. Do you want me to tie you to the back of the wagon with the cow?"

Brownie came back to the wagon, but the other hound took off down the road. He was baying each time he hit the ground. Tom said, "Surely someone lives nearby. That hound is telling them that company is coming."

Soon the wagon came around a curve in the road. Tom could see a cabin in the distance. A woman and a young man stood in front of the cabin. Tom recognized them as Catherine and George Washington.

He stood up in the wagon and tapped the horses with the reins. This was the first time in over five hundred miles of travel that Tom's horses had felt a whip. They responded, and the wagon bounced down the road. Both little girls laughed loudly.

Catherine and George Washington had also recognized Tom. They started running toward the wagon. Soon they met. Catherine was laughing and crying at the same time. "Oh, Tom, Tom, Tom. Let me see those babies! Girls, girls. Oh, you precious babies! They look just like Margaret did when she was a baby, but they are so alike. Which is which, Tom?"

"The one on the right is Julia Anna, and the one on the left is Margaret Emily." And from that day forward, with a grandmother's wisdom, Catherine could always tell the twins apart.

George Washington shook hands with Tom. Tom said, "George, you're not Katie's little brother now. Looks like you've grown up."

"I'm already thirteen. I can do a man's work now. I'll take the horses and unhitch and feed them. I'll take care of the cow, too."

"Go on over and tell Isaac and Elizabeth that Tom and the twins are here," Catherine told George.

Tom and Catherine took the twins and went on into the house. Catherine was beside herself with happiness! Yet, she could not help shedding a few tears for Katie, whose death still seemed so untimely. She and Tom had much to talk about. They put Julia Anna and Margaret Emily on the floor, and Tom went into the kitchen for a drink of water. Catherine checked on a potful of beans that were cooking for supper.

Imagine Tom's surprise when he returned to the main room of the cabin. Julia Anna and Margaret Emily were both standing. They both headed toward Tom with faltering steps, and each of them said, "Pa."

"Well, well," said Tom. "We just got to your grandma's house, and both of you start walking and talking. At the same time, of course. Looks like you are showing off for your grandma." Tom's expression showed how proud he was of those little girls!

By that time George was back home, accompanied by Isaac and Elizabeth and their two children. The little family group was happy to be together. They found themselves all talking at once.

Elizabeth said, "Mother Davis, I'll finish supper. You enjoy your grandchildren."

"That's an offer I won't refuse," Catherine said as she gathered her little brood in her arms.

Five-year-old William said, "There's two of them, and they are just alike. But I'm lots bigger."

The adults laughed.

When supper was ready, the family all sat down to eat. Catherine said, "Tom, ask the blessing."

"God in Heaven, thank You for bringing us safely all the way to this home. Keep us in Thy care."

"Amen," chorused the others who were at the table.

The evening passed quickly. Tom had to admit that he was looking forward to sleeping in a real bed again after spending over three months sleeping on the ground.

During the next two days Tom looked over the area around Fox Creek and visited with neighbors, the Fields, Todds, and Upshaws. He felt right at home. The Ozarks were much like the area of Indiana that he had always called home.

Chapter 15

A Blacksmith Shop in the Ozarks

Tom loaded a batching outfit in his wagon. His blacksmith tools which he had brought from Indiana were already in the wagon.

Catherine was happy to keep the twins for as long as Tom needed her to do so. Tom didn't realize that it would be so difficult to say goodbye to the twins for even a few days. He assured them and Catherine that he would be back by the end of the next week. Then he got into his wagon and headed back in a westerly direction, looking for a place to settle. On the previous day he had decided that the most desirable places along Fox Creek were already settled. He told Catherine and Isaac, "The area over on Bryant Creek looked good to me. Not as many people have settled there. There seemed to be an abundance of pine trees that would make good logs for buildings. The bluestem grass was lush and would feed plenty of stock. The streams were clear and flowed freely. I'll head over that way. Seemed like I was somewhat drawn to that creek."

By evening Tom was on Bryant Creek. He discovered a cave with a large entrance. He pulled his wagon near the entrance and made camp there. The arrowheads, spear points, and scrapers that his keen eyes saw told him that Indians had once occupied this cave.

The next morning he left his wagon, supplies, and workhorses at the cave. He had already decided to use this cave as a permanent campsite. Riding his saddle horse, Tom went up Bryant Creek to a little settlement called Red Bud. It pleased and surprised Tom to find a gristmill there. He visited with the Hicks, Wilson, Sloan, and Coats families. They all told him the same thing. There was not a single blacksmith shop in the whole area. One was badly needed, they all agreed. All of them predicted more settlers and more growth in the area. Roads would be built. Schools and churches were needed and would be built. Tom told them about the three families that had come with him.

Late in the afternoon Tom returned to his camp in the cave. He was surprised when he found himself thinking of it as "home." The men whom he had met all assured him that they would help him build a shop and a cabin. They all said that they enjoyed log rollings and cabin raisings. The prospect of having a blacksmith shop in the area pleased everyone.

The next morning Tom went down the creek to another settlement called Rockbridge. Again every man that he met assured him that the area was in dire need of a blacksmith shop.

Tom returned to his home camp that night. The call of a whippoorwill, "whip-whip-whip-er-will," made him realize how much he missed his babies. "Nothing is more lonesome than the sound of that bird's cry," Tom said. "And nothing raises a man's spirits as much as catching a fish," he added. He went down to the creek that was only a few feet from the mouth of the cave. Soon he had caught a couple of nice perch. He quickly cleaned them and put them in his iron skillet to cook. As they cooked, he thought, "I've explored up and down Bryant Creek. I like this place better than anything that I have seen. I will camp here while I build my shop. Then I will build a cabin. I've found good locations for both. There's a level spot just above the cave. I'll build my shop there. Tomorrow I'll start cutting the logs. But tomorrow is Saturday, so I'll quit early and head toward Fox Creek to see my girls. Wonder if they have missed their old pa?"

The next few weeks passed quickly . . . almost routinely. Tom cut and hewed the straight pine trees into logs for his shop. He cut a nice pile of clapboards for the roof. How thankful he was that he had brought his tools from Indiana!

On Saturday afternoon he was ready to go see his girls, his Julia Anna and Margaret Emily. When he got to their grandma's home, she told him that some of the neighbors were getting together for church services the next day in the Joseph Todd home. They had asked if Tom would preach. "I took the liberty of telling them that you would," Catherine said.

"Yes, I want to," Tom replied. "It will be good to worship together. That will really make this seem like home."

Immediately a scripture from Deuteronomy

came to Tom's mind. "For the Lord thy God bringeth thee into a good land, a land of brooks of water, of fountains and depths that spring out of the valleys and hills; a land of wheat and barley and vines . . . a land of honey."

Tom looked at his twins. He watched their doting grandmother as she noticed every move, every faltering step, that the babies made. He thought, "Sounds like God was describing the Ozarks. I believe that He brought my babies and me here." He knew what his subject would be for the next day's sermon.

On Sunday evening both Isaac and George Washington accompanied Tom back to his camp. Monday morning, neighbors were coming. Tom was ready for a cabin raisin'. The cabin would be his blacksmith shop.

The finished shop would be about sixteen feet wide by twenty feet long. "A shop must have enough room for a man to work," Tom told the men. He had already found four big flat rocks for cornerstones, and they were in place.

The cabin grew by pairs of logs; two on the sides, followed by two on the ends, and so on. The lower notches of each new log rested on the upper ones of the preceding pair. Tom explained to the men who were helping him, "A shop needs to be a little taller than a cabin." When the shop was as high as Tom thought it needed to be, the men put on the log called the ridge pole. It would support the roof.

The next day Tom and his brothers-in-law roofed the shop. Tom had the clapboards ready for this. The gable ends were put on, and the shop was ready for the finishing touches. Tom appreciated all the help he had gotten, but he wanted to do the final little jobs by himself. He thanked Isaac and George for their help, and they went on back to their own homes on Fox Creek. "Give the girls a big hug from their pa. Tell Catherine and them that I'll see them on Saturday night."

Wednesday morning Tom was at his new shop building ready to work before the sun peeked over the eastern horizon. He could not wait to start building his forge. He said to himself, "The forge, not the building, makes a blacksmith shop." He carefully stacked rocks until they were about two and a half feet high. He used mortar that he had made to hold the rocks together. Then he made a fire hole a little in front of the center. An iron grate, which he had brought from his shop in Indiana, was set in this hole to hold the charcoal. The ash pit was below the grate.

When the forge was finished, Tom looked at it with pride. He was ready to make the bellows. How happy he was that he had brought well-tanned deer skins for this. The bellows must be able to expel enough air to blow the fire. Tom smiled and hummed a tune as he worked. "It's easier now to understand why there is no blacksmith shop in the area. I'm glad that I know what I'm doing. Experience really is the best teacher."

The bellows were finished and ready to use. Then Tom placed his anvil on the huge butt of a log that he put on the earthen floor about four feet in front of the forge. He brought in his tongs and the iron that he had brought from Indiana.

"The Bryant Creek area in Ozark County has its first blacksmith shop. The smithy, Tom Brown, is ready to work. There's not a thing made out of iron that I can't make," Tom laughed. But, oh, he was pleased that his shop was ready to use, ready for the business of helping his neighbor. It was Saturday night. He must get on his way. Julia Anna and Margaret Emily would be waiting for him.

Monday morning he would work in his shop. He needed to think about getting a cabin ready to live in.

Chapter 16

The Year of 1845 Ends

October was beautiful in the Ozarks. Tom had never seen such vivid color in maple, sassafras, wild cherry, sycamore, ash, and oak trees. The pines were so thick and green that they looked black in the distance. This was the time of the year that was called "Indian summer."

As much as Tom enjoyed the October weather, he knew that he must work every possible minute and get his cabin built. More and more people were showing up at his blacksmith shop with work for him to do. Word of his shop had spread in all directions. He was amazed when he heard how far some of the men had traveled to get to his shop. "People of the Ozarks need my services," he said to himself.

The weekdays passed quickly. Each Saturday evening Tom made the journey to the Davis home on Fox Creek. He missed the twins too much to be away from them more than a week at a time. Their laughter when they saw their pa convinced him that each trip was worth the time and effort that it took.

Tom complained to Catherine that he could not seem to get much done toward building his cabin. She saw that he was a little frustrated because of this. "The corn here is gathered, and George and Isaac have laid in my winter's wood. I can get by here with the twins. Isaac and Elizabeth are nearby to help me. Why don't you take George back with you? He could help you until about Thanksgiving."

"The hogs will be fat and ready to butcher by Thanksgiving. I've got one for you, Tom. Elizabeth and I will render your lard and make your sausage. Just be sure that George is back by Thanksgiving. Maybe you could help with the butchering, too."

"I'll plan to," Tom assured her. "I'll bring my big kettle." He smiled to himself as he remembered buying the kettle in Indiana. He thought of the "nest" which he had made in the kettle. Each of the twins had ridden part of the way to Missouri in that iron kettle. He said, "Oh, the tales that I'll tell my girls about their journey to the Ozarks . . . their ride in the old iron kettle."

So George went home with Tom. George was surprised to see how comfortable the cave was. "Maybe you should just forget building a cabin and live in this cave, Tom," George said.

"I'm a man, not a mole, George. A man needs a cabin."

George was good help. By the middle of November they had cut enough logs to build a cabin. Tom put the sections of logs that he used to make clapboards near his shop. He kept his froe handy. When he had a little time between jobs in the shop, he split out a few more clapboards. He was surprised to see how fast his stack of finished clapboards grew. The yellow pine was easy to work with. The grain was straight, and there was hardly ever a knot.

On the second weekend in November Tom took George back to his home. While Tom was there, they made plans to butcher on the Wednesday before Thanksgiving. Tom said, "I won't come again until then." The week before Thanksgiving Tom told the men who came to his shop about his plans. He didn't want to leave his shop without an explanation. He also passed the word that his logs were cut. He was ready for another cabin raising. This time the cabin was to live in . . . his home in the Ozarks. The date set for the cabin raising was for the Monday after Thanksgiving.

He told each man, "I owe you a day's work. I'll pay you with shop work or any way you choose. I don't want to be in debt or beholden to anyone." Each man assured Tom that they were so glad to have a blacksmith shop in the area that he was beholden to no one.

"Besides," said old Jerry Coats, "that's the way we do here in the Ozarks. We help our neighbor."

Tom started to the Davis home on Tuesday afternoon. On the way he killed a young deer and a wild turkey. When he got to Catherine's home, he said, "Well, I'm not an Indian, but I brought Thanksgiving dinner. Didn't the Indians take turkeys and deer to the first feast with the Pilgrims?"

"Oh, Tom, you beat all!" Catherine said. "But

it will be good to have turkey for Thanksgiving dinner."

Julia Anna and Margaret Emily chorused together, "See, see."

George helped Tom clean and dress the turkey and the deer. For supper they had fresh venison steaks.

The day before Thanksgiving they butchered six hogs. Pork was the main food in their diet. The men did the actual killing of the hogs, a job Tom never learned to enjoy. Then each hog had to be scalded and all of the bristles or hair scraped off the hide.

Tom said, "I brought my hunting knife and an extra butcher knife. They are both sharp. A man needs the right kind of tool to do any job. They need to be in the best possible shape."

"Right, Tom. We knew that we could depend on you for sharp knives."

When the hogs were scraped, they were hung by their hind legs in a tree and cut open. Then the insides were taken out.

Catherine and Elizabeth washed the hearts and livers and put them carefully aside. They saved all the bits of fat to make lard. The men then cut each hog into halves. By Friday the halves would be cold and ready to cut into hams, shoulders, and sides of bacon. These would be salted and put into the smokehouse to cure. Later a small hickory fire would smolder in the smokehouse for days, and the meat would all be smoked. It would then keep throughout the hot summer and not spoil.

Butchering day was a long, hard day for the men. Then days of work for Catherine and Elizabeth began. Sausage, headcheese, and souse had to be made. Lard had to be rendered. Nothing was wasted. After the lard was rendered, a supply of soap for the coming year needed to be made. Catherine already had the lye that she had made from the ashes which she had put through the lye hopper.

They did not work on Thanksgiving Day. That was the day for giving thanks and for feasting. Tom loved the feasting. He looked at his twins and said, "I have much for which I am thankful." Then he added, "Um, um, um. Nothing tastes as good as fresh pork!"

Butchering for the year was done. They would all have meat for the next year.

Tom spent the rest of the week enjoying being with his twins. He held them on his knees by the hour, singing to them and telling them stories.

On Sunday evening Isaac and George accompanied Tom back to his cave home. On Monday the men from up and down Bryant Creek would be there for a cabin raising. Tom said, "A real roof over my head. A roof made of clapboards and logs instead of the solid rock of the cave."

During December Tom worked at finishing the cabin. James Wilson had a gristmill and a sawmill on Hunter Creek near the spot where Hunter emptied into Bryant. Mr. Wilson had helped when the neighbors met to raise Tom's cabin. He had told Tom that he had some extra lumber sawed.

Tom decided to take his wagon and go to Wilson's mill for lumber to floor the cabin. He thought, "I'll get enough lumber for a floor and a loft. I could get by without a loft for the present, but one would make the cabin look so much better. A loft would make it warmer in winter and cooler in summer, and it would be a good storage place. I'll need to have a place to keep vegetables such as onions and pumpkins—a place where they won't freeze in the winter. And, who knows, there may be another wife in my future. I will need someone to care for Margaret Emily and Julia Anna when I bring them home. Yes, I will put a loft in my cabin."

He built the fireplace out of rocks. After the fireplace was finished, he started working on a wide mantle board. While he worked on the mantle, he slipped back into his habit of pondering, thinking, remembering, and pondering some more. Often his thoughts returned to Indiana . . . to the lonely hill and the two graves on it . . . to the old Shiloh Methodist Church . . . to Nashville. He thought of the Floyds and the Hamptons. He wished he knew about Hannah's baby.

Many times each day he thought of Julia Anna and Margaret Emily and of how much he missed them each night. How happy he would be when he could have them with him. He would take them back to see their grandmother often and let them stay with her some of the time. She would remain an important part of their lives, but he wanted to raise them.

When the mantle was finished and in place, Tom carefully unpacked the clock—the one that Katie had taken such pride in. He placed it on the mantle. Next he put his Bible by the clock. Then he hung his rifle on the pegs that he had put into the logs above the mantle. He stood back and looked. A pleased expression covered his entire face. "Welcome home, Tom," he said to himself. "Home. Your home in the Ozarks just across Bryant Creek from your blacksmith shop."

Tom was always busy, so he set to work making

119

the furniture for his cabin. First he made the bed. Robert Hicks and his family lived at Red Bud, about three miles up the creek from Tom. He had told Tom about the good wheat crop that he had raised that year. Mr. Hicks needed his wagon wheels rebuilt. Tom said, "I'll fix your wheel for enough straw to fill my straw ticks. I have built my bed, and I need to get a straw mattress on it." The trade was made.

Tom had brought his bedding, pewter dishes,

iron pots, and two cane-bottomed chairs from Indiana.
He put the chairs in front of the fireplace. The table and
two benches that he had made were placed by the wall.
Looking around the cabin, he was pleased with what he
saw. "Not bad, not bad. Could use a woman's touch,
but not bad. Not bad at all."

The cabin was finished and furnished.

Christmas was only a few days away. Tom was not very busy in his shop. He felt that he could give George a few lessons in hunting and trapping. Isaac had a yoke of oxen to break. Tom told himself that he could help with that. He could think of several good reasons to spend time with the Davis family. But the best, the most important reason, was that his twins would have their first birthday on Christmas Day. He must be with them for that special day.

So Tom spent the week before Christmas on Fox Creek with his kin doing family things. He did a number of chores for Catherine, his mother-in-law and the grandmother of his babies. "She has been so good and kind to me. She loves the babies with all of her heart," he said to himself.

Young George and Tom went hunting and trapping. Tom thought, "George is a big boy. Big enough to be a man. Yet, he is still a boy at heart. He has grown up without a father. I must spend more time with him. He seems so interested in the blacksmith shop work. I'll see if he would like to learn the trade. He is going to have the size and strength for it."

Isaac and Tom enjoyed the time that they spent together. A widow, Elizabeth Dodson, lived near the Davis family. She had two young yearling calves that Tom bought. He named them Red and Patch. The names fit. He would need oxen come spring.

Isaac and Tom made a small yoke for Tom's calves and a larger yoke for Isaac's oxen. They worked

gently with the oxen to train them. Tom warned Isaac, "We can ruin them if we don't break them in right."

"Uncle Tom, can I help? Can I?" asked William.

"Course you can help, William. You're almost six now, aren't you?" answered Tom.

"And can I go hunting with you and Uncle George? Can I?" William begged. Tom and Isaac laughed.

As they sat around the fireplace at night, Tom was busy on another project. When he made the table for his cabin, he had made a small table for the twins. Now he was making three little chairs to go with that table. Two for his girls and one for Isaac and Elizabeth's little Sarilda Jane. She and her little cousins played together. Tom thought, "These little chairs and the table will be my birthday present for the girls."

Christmas Day came. Isaac, Elizabeth, William, and Sarilda Jane spent the day with Catherine, George Washington, Tom, and the twins. It was good to be together as a family. Yet, each of the adults felt an emptiness, a loneliness, as they remembered Katie. Each of them thought of her differently . . . wife, daughter, sister. But they all thought, "Mother of Julia Anna and Margaret Emily, two precious little girls."

Those two little girls and their cousin, Sarilda Jane, brought laughter to the cabin. "Just listen to them! I can't understand a thing that they are saying, can you?" Catherine, the doting grandmother, said.

Tom laughed, "I can't either. But they understand each other. That's plain to see."

Everyone enjoyed the Christmas dinner that Catherine and Elizabeth had prepared.

"Everything was so good, but I've never eaten anything that was better than that persimmon pudding," Tom said. He rubbed his stomach that was obviously too full.

"And I gathered the persimmons and picked out the hickory nuts for it," William reminded them all.

That afternoon the adults sat around the fireplace. They talked and watched the three little girls play. William cracked and picked out more hickory nuts. Tom said, "Maybe we could have another persimmon pudding for New Year's dinner."

"If I can beat the possums to the persimmons and if Grandma will make it, we can," William assured him.

Tom was hesitant to bring up the subject, but he said, "Over on Bryant Creek not far from my shop there is a family named Burdan. They're all good people. They have a daughter named Mary, but everyone calls her Polly. She's eighteen years old and just as nice as she can be . . ."

Catherine saw that Tom was struggling with what he was trying to tell them. She added, "So, you've gotten acquainted with Mary, or Polly, as you say she is called. You've been talking to her."

"Yes," Tom said. Then he hastily added before he lost his nerve, "We have talked of marrying. I'd like to bring her to see the twins." He looked at them, and a tear slid from his eyes. "My Julia Anna and Margaret Emily, I think she would be a good mother for them."

"I know you can't go on living alone, Tom. A man needs a wife," Catherine said.

Tom breathed a sigh of relief. "Silly for a man who is over thirty years old to be embarrassed," he thought.

Plans were made for Tom to bring Polly for dinner on New Year's Day.

"And I will find enough persimmons for a pudding, Uncle Tom. If I have to hunt through the woods for miles around, I'll do it," added William.

They saw that the little girls, Margaret Emily,

Julia Anna, and Sarilda Jane, were tired. Tom picked up his girls and put one on each knee. Isaac picked up Sarilda Jane.

Tom began to sing softly.

> "Silent Night, Holy Night
> All is calm, all is bright . . ."

And Christmas—Christmas with its "Peace on earth and good will toward men"—settled on that little family group in their log home in the Ozarks. Christmas of 1845.

Epilogue

Every family has its own stories and traditions. This book comes from our Brown family stories which have been passed down from one generation to another for over one hundred fifty years.

My grandsons are five generations removed from Thomas S. Brown. Nothing thrills me more than to have one of them crawl up beside me and say, "Tell me a story about the old days." That is what I have attempted to do in this book that is based on family history woven together with imagination.

Many of the people, incidents, and places that I have written about are from the pages of our family history. Tom did camp the winter of 1844–45 in the cave on Bryant Creek. This cave today is called Brown's Cave. He did build the first blacksmith shop that was in the area.

Thomas S. Brown was born in Virginia in 1814. He married Sarah Floyd, who died shortly afterward. Then he married Margaret (Katie) Davis. Her twins, Julia Anna and Margaret Emily, were born on Christmas Day 1844. Katie died in childbirth, but both babies lived. Tom brought them to the Ozarks in 1845. Both of them were married twice and reared families by each husband. Julia Anna married Louis Gardner. A son, Parrot, was born in 1863. Louis died in 1874. Later Julia Anna married John R. Gaulding, and they reared three children. Margaret Emily was the mother of twelve children. She and her first husband, Andrew Gaulding, had nine children. After Andrew's death she married Moses T. Winn, and they had three children. Both Julia Anna and Margaret Emily died in the month of May. Julia Anna died in 1919 at the age of seventy-four, and Margaret Emily died four years later. They are buried near each other in the Gaulding family cemetery in Ozark County, Missouri.

Tom did bring a big, black, iron kettle to the Ozarks with him. Tom told the story of the kettle to his son, Edward. Edward was the youngest of seven children born to Thomas S. and Mary Burden, whom Tom married on February 27, 1846, in Ozark County, Missouri. Edward told the kettle story to his son Walter. Walter passed the kettle and the story on to his son Logan, my husband. The kettle sits by our fireplace today. It will be passed on down to one of our grandsons, and they must know its story.